ABI AND THE BOY SHE LOVES

KELSIE STELTING

D1519524

CONTENTS

THIS WAS EXACTLY where Jon belonged. On the track, the wind he created flying through his hair, his face determined, his lungs heaving, his muscles rippling with every labored step.

My cheers for him blended with his parents', Grandma's, Jorge's, and everyone else there to support the runners at the first indoor meet of the season. Each lap they made with Jon edging steadily ahead only reinforced how invested he was in this sport. How right the coaches had been to recruit him.

The closer he and his competitors got to the end, the louder the entire place grew until all I could hear was an echoing of yells and claps. I watched his feet, barely touching the ground before lifting and pressing forward. Ahead.

He crossed the finish line at the front of the pack. His steps slowed, but his chest lifted and fell rapidly. He laced his fingers behind his head and sucked in big gasps for air. As sweat slicked his skin, I thought he had never looked more beautiful.

Not like the photo Marta snapped of me after my race. My skin was ruddy, and my frizzy hair was desperately attempting to escape my ponytail. It wasn't fair. But then again, I didn't have to look at myself until I'd had a good shower. I could keep taking in the sight of Jon all day long, though.

I probably should put my tongue back in my mouth before someone slipped on my drool and got hurt. But still. Damn.

I absently scratched at my shoulder, then stopped myself. My skin was healing, which only meant the scabs itched like crazy. Especially with the dried sweat irritating it. I was so ready for a good shower and a dinner out with our families.

I waited in the stands with them while the awards ceremony took place. I hadn't won any of my events, but I hadn't placed last either. For me, that was the same as winning, and for the first meet of the season, I was thankful to just be...average. For once. It meant I belonged here too. I wasn't just a charity case anymore; I was a part of the team.

But Jon stood out on the platform as they placed a medal around his neck. The corners of his lips tugged against a smile as he tried acting like he wasn't over-the-moon excited about his win.

When we finished clapping and cheering, I leaned over to the others and said, "I'm going to the team meeting, and then I'll take a quick shower."

Marta smiled at me. "Take your time, sweetie. Our dinner reservation isn't 'til six."

The watch on my wrist said we were still an hour and a half off, which royally stunk. I was starving.

Turned out, a girl could get used to eating more. And still do well in college track.

Grandma stood up and gave me a tight squeeze.

"I'm going to get you all sweaty!" I cried.

She held on even tighter. "It's worth it. I'm so proud of you."

I hugged her back and said, "Thank you," even though the words didn't convey enough. I wouldn't be here without her.

I went down to the place where the girls' distance team was supposed to meet and sat on the floor beside Nikki. She was absently stretching, not really putting too much effort into it.

"You did awesome today," I said.

She smiled. "It wasn't first."

"It wasn't last either," I said. "Second place isn't anything to turn your nose up at."

She pushed the end of her nose up and snorted like a pig.

I shoved her shoulder, laughing.

"Okay, ladies," Coach Cadence said, silencing us and our teammates. "We had a good first meet today. We placed sixth as a team, which is very promising for our season."

We let out a few exhausted whoops, and she smiled until we quieted down.

She went around the group, offering congratulations and quick pieces of advice, but she skipped me.

"Go shower up," she said. And then she added, "Abi, can you stay behind?"

I nodded, not wanting to meet her eyes. I'd been happy with how I ran, but now I wondered if I should be worried. Had I done something wrong?

As the other girls left, I stood up to face whatever Coach Cadence had to say to me.

"How are you doing?" she asked.

"Good?" I eyed her, waiting for the real reason she asked me to stay behind.

Her chocolate eyes were softer now. "I know you've had a hard start to your semester, but I'm proud of how far you've come, and you should be too."

Relief flooded my chest, making my heart buoy so high I worried it might float away. My lightweight sneakers wouldn't do anything to keep the rest of me on the ground. "You mean it?"

With a smile, she nodded. "You've worked hard to get better, both on the track and up here." She tapped her forehead.

I just nodded because weekly therapy sessions hadn't been easy. My therapist dug through the darkest corners of my mind—of my past—and worked with all the painful memories until I was exhausted in every sense of the word. It was all I could do to go back to my dorm and curl up for a nap afterwards.

"Now, go shower up." She nodded toward the stands where I'd been sitting with Jon's parents, Grandma, and Jorge. "It looks like you've got some fans waiting to celebrate you."

"Thanks, Coach," I said.

My smile was still on my face as I showered, changed, and met the others in the stands. Jon was nowhere to be seen, so I guessed he was still getting cleaned up.

Grandma gripped my arm. "Can you show me where the bathroom is?"

"Sure." We walked through the thinning crowd to a bathroom. I stood off to the side to wait for Grandma, but she stopped beside me.

"We need to talk."

I girded my heart as I stepped closer to the cinderblock wall, away from the other people walking by. "What's going on? Are you okay?"

My mind was going to all the horrible places. Cancer. Disease. Financial struggles. I needed her to just tell me so I could quit imagining every terrible scenario.

"Your father is up for parole."

CHAPTER TWO

IN ALL THE situations I'd imagined, that was not one of them.

I stumbled back until I was fully leaning against the wall. "They said ten years in prison."

"Texas prisons are overcrowded." Her voice had a pained tone, like she hated that fact as much as a person could. "They're trying to clear out non-violent offenders, and your father's had good behavior."

Good behavior? Non-violent? "What about the hit and run where a girl died and her boyfriend nearly killed me?" I demanded, already feeling the familiar rush of adrenaline and stress saturate my system. Blood heated in my veins, boiling to the surface.

"The police reviewed the evidence last week and said there wasn't enough to substantiate that it was him."

Another blow. "You didn't tell me that."

She looked toward the ground. "I thought you had enough to worry about."

"I do now." I raked my fingers through my still-wet hair and scratched at the base of my ponytail.

Grandma put a hand on my shoulder, trying to steady me, but it only agitated my itching skin and set me more on edge.

Dad was getting out of prison. *Could be* getting out of prison.

Any time I'd allowed my mind to go to that place, I'd imagined it being ten years in the future. That was long enough for me to have a job. Be settled with a family. Have plans in place and security systems on alert, in case something were to happen.

But now? I felt just as vulnerable as I had been running through that pasture with Eric gunning the engine behind me. There were some things I couldn't outrun. I'd gotten lucky back there. So incredibly lucky.

Would that same kind of fortune strike again?

"I—I need—" I stalled. What did I need? Other than new parents or for mine to be in jail, unable to harm me, for the rest of their lives? "I need to find Jon."

I started away from Grandma, going back toward the locker rooms. I fished my phone out of my pocket, dialed his number.

I'd made a promise to Jon that I would tell him what was going on, and even though part of me was screaming to separate this messy part of my life from the life I wanted to live with him, I knew I couldn't. The past had made me who I was, and Jon wanted me. All of me.

I heard Jon's ringtone before I saw him coming out of the locker room, reaching into his gym bag.

"Jon," I said, hanging up.

He smiled at me, but his face immediately fell at my expression. "What's wrong?" He hurried to me, and his hands went to my face, his eyes searching me for signs of trouble. "Are you okay?"

I shook my head, seconds from falling apart. "My dad might be getting out of prison. He's up for parole."

I sobbed into Jon's chest, and he let his bag drop to the floor so he could wrap his arms around me, hold me tight.

"Abi," he said, his voice firm. He took my arms,

gripping them, and met my eyes. "I will keep you safe. I promise."

I could tell he meant every word. "But how?"

We weren't allowed to have guns on campus. All the self-defense items I'd bought hadn't done a lick of good against Eric when I'd tried to outrun his pickup. Dad was a big man, outweighing Jon by at least a hundred pounds. What chance did he or I have?

He pulled back and held my face in his hands. With steel in his eyes and iron in his voice, he said, "However I need to. I will *not* let anyone else hurt you."

I believed him. But as we walked to meet our families, it hit me: he'd made no promises about keeping himself safe in the process.

We were too close to them now for me to say anything, so I just squeezed his hand a little tighter. Loved him a little harder. Jon wouldn't think of himself when it came down to it—only the people he loved.

I could have held on forever, but his parents greeted him with all the enthusiasm a first-place finish deserved. I watched his face light up as they congratulated him, wishing I could always see that joy there. College was hard though—we had plenty of late-night study sessions, homework dates that turned into recovery breakfasts before track practice. But we also had each other.

Pride still gleaming in her eyes, Marta said, "We have reservations. Are you ready?"

Jon nodded and wrapped his arm around me. I was secure once again.

We all walked outside, but Marta offered for her and Glen to go get the vehicle. I tried not to be bothered by the grateful look on Grandma's face. Since when was she not up for a walk?

Glen saluted us. "Be back in a bit."

The four of us—Grandma, Jorge, Jon and I—stood around in silence for a moment. Jon moved behind me, resting his chin on my head, and I leaned back against him.

"That was quite a race," Jorge said, to Jon I knew.

"Thanks," Jon said. "We've been training hard."

"It shows."

Grandma nodded in agreement. "Abi said how busy the two of you have been. I bet you're going to be ready for a break come Christmastime."

Jon held me a little tighter. "You have no idea."

CHAPTER THREE

THEY DROPPED us off at the dorms around eight o'clock since Jon and I had homework to get done for classes Monday. Because Kyle had an out-of-town game and Jon's dorm was empty, we went up there and got started on our assignments.

He sat at his desk, and I dropped my backpack on the futon, which had to be a million years old. I probably wouldn't feel safe sitting on it, honestly, if Kyle and Anika weren't so set on abstinence.

As I relaxed back, coils squealed underneath me. A small, niggling part of my brain immediately blamed my weight, but I caught myself mid-spiral, like my therapist had taught me.

No more building the case against myself.

No, it was this stupid futon that needed to be replaced.

"You tired?" Jon asked.

I shook my head, focusing my gaze on him. "No. I mean, yeah, but that's not it."

He lifted a corner of his lips in a concerned half smile, half frown. "Worried about your dad?"

That wasn't it, but the news of his potential parole hadn't helped all these loud, negative thoughts. It was like my mind was a beehive, and any mention of my parents was a bear swiping its paw at the nest. I needed time to settle.

Jon took my silence for an affirmation and said, "Your grandma said the actual parole hearing isn't for months. We might be worried about nothing."

I met his eyes, held on to the hope taking residence there. "Maybe." I let my fears stay silent inside my mind, thinking we could be worried for exactly the right reason. My father wasn't one to let wrongs go unpunished.

"Maybe I could do something to distract you?" He stood up from the desk and came over to the futon, straddling my legs with his, my shoulders with his arms. There was a fiery look in his eyes I never got tired of seeing.

I lifted my chin, putting my lips only inches from his. "Yeah?" I breathed. "What's your idea?"

He smirked. "I was thinking something like..." He pressed his lips to mine. One second. Two seconds. Enough to make the oxygen flee from my head. "How's that?"

I swallowed. "Not bad, Scoller."

His smile turned wicked. "I wasn't going for 'not bad.'"

"Well then." I quirked a brow. "You need to step up your game."

"Challenge accepted." His breath tickled my skin, but soon his perfectly soft lips were feathering kisses at the base of my neck, up to my chin, the dip below my ear, nibbling on my earlobe—I gasped at the tingle that ran through my body.

That only encouraged him.

The kisses became faster until we were breathless and my dad was the farthest thing from my mind.

He pulled back, his eyes still ablaze. "How was that?"

"Flawless," I breathed.

When he replied, his voice was soft, his smile playful. "I aim to please."

As if he could do anything else. I was supposed

to take Jon off the pedestal, but come on. He was Jon. And I was only human.

Now, he got off the couch, and I pulled at his jacket, whining.

He danced away from my grasp. "We need to get our homework done before you can distract me any more than you already have."

"Later?" I asked.

"Duh."

I laughed and bent to my backpack. I had a policy class to study for. Our teacher was having us memorize countless supreme court cases, and I needed my grade to be good for my law school applications.

Using index cards and brand-new markers Grandma sent in a care package, I began writing each case and the main points I needed to know. Getting lost in this was easy—something about one decision impacting people for generations to come spoke to me. Someday, I wanted to help people get these decisions right.

Jon let out a heavy sigh. The kind you usually only heard from old men talking about millennials.

My hand froze on Griswold vs. Connecticut. "Everything okay?"

He let out another groan in response and pushed back from his desk.

"You're going full-blown caveman; it must be bad."

Not even a hint of humor touched his face. Instead, he pressed the heels of his hands into his eyes and slowly rubbed.

I stood from the chair, setting down my notes. "What's going on?"

Refusing to speak, he gestured at the computer screen, where there was a handwritten note on a scanned document.

Lacks personality. There has to be more to you than running, Mr. Gump.

My eyebrows flew up my forehead. "Your professor wrote that?"

"Yep," Jon said flatly. "On my personal profile paper."

I couldn't imagine some backward scenario where a professor had the gall to say something like that to a student. Much less one like Jon. "For what class?"

"Human behavior."

"That's so inappropriate," I said.

Jon ran his hands over his face. "He said I need to do it over or I'll keep the D minus he gave me."

"D minus?"

"Yep."

I hated that word now. *Yep*. And the professor who made Jon say it in such a dejected way. Didn't he know Jon was the hardest working person in existence? That he poured his heart and soul and body into track practices to be the very best he could be? How could the professor minimize that into a poorly constructed *Forrest Gump* reference? The more I thought about it, the more I hated the guy.

"I can go tell him exactly where to shove his D minus," I grumbled.

Jon cast me a sideways glance. "Maybe we shouldn't be talking about professors shoving their Ds places."

"Oh God." My cheeks went immediately red, and I covered my face with my hands.

At last, I heard Jon laugh, but the tightness in my chest remained.

CHAPTER FOUR

I THINK I finally understood the creeps in vampire movies. I woke up before Jon the next morning, and for a while, I just watched him sleep. He looked so peaceful like this.

Sometimes, I felt like I needed to steal his peace for myself. I didn't have much lately. Even though the letters had stopped and Grandma said Eric was still in the hospital, I didn't feel safe on campus. Or anywhere, really.

Only when I was right next to Jon. Or Anika. Or Nikki.

I didn't trust myself to meet anyone new, especially when my radar had been so off with Eric. But I *knew* Jon in every way a person could know someone. I wanted to keep knowing him forever.

He shifted, and his arm tightened around me. I froze, hoping he would stay asleep and I could watch him a while longer.

When he slept like this, he looked younger, care-free, his dark lashes fanned across his cheeks and the corners of his mouth slack.

I still couldn't believe the professor had told Jon he didn't have a personality. But then I remembered Jon's past abuse from his mom's boyfriend. He seemed so well-adjusted it was easy to forget he carried scars of his own.

I hadn't read the paper, but maybe his bland presentation of himself was his scar tissue. Some-times, when you're hurt, you don't want to lay your-self bare. You can't. You hide yourself behind a thick, protective barrier. The more someone knew about you, the more they could hold against you.

My mom was proof of that.

She might not know me anymore, but she knew the deepest corners of my insecurities and wielded them better than any weapon. Eric knew where I came from, the monster of a man whose blood ran through my veins, and he persecuted me for that.

The ways they'd attacked me made me feel even luckier that I had friends at home who cared for me. Who I could trust.

I couldn't wait to see them over Christmas break. Especially Skye, Andrew, and Roberto. The East Coast was too far away. I missed them and having all of our friends together.

Jon shifted again, but this time, one of his eyes opened. "Are you staring at me?"

Slightly embarrassed, I said, "So what if I am?"

"Then I'll have to give you something to stare at."

"What does that mean?"

"I don't know," he huffed and scooted closer. "Now, shut up and kiss me."

We stayed in bed, kissing, enjoying each other until my stomach was growling and Jon was insisting we go to the dining hall. I didn't want to leave though. I wanted to stay in this safe nest blanketed in the love we'd created.

"Kyle's going to be here soon anyway," Jon reminded me. "Might as well give him some time to settle in."

"Yeah," I agreed, even though I didn't want to.

We stopped by my room so I could change and brush my teeth, then continued to the dining hall. The other reason I didn't like going out? Everyone stared at me now. I'd barely gotten used to the forced anonymity college offered, and now I was a local celebrity. But in the sad, kitten-you-can't-adopt-staring-at-you-from-behind-the-cage kind of way. Everyone wanted to know how I'd escaped Eric's attack two months ago. What I'd done to earn such a wrath. Why the guy in news stories had gone from cute and rugged to vicious and bandaged in a hospital bed.

"I hate this," I muttered after the person swiping us in stared at me for way too long.

Jon held on tighter to my waist. "It's not your problem. It's theirs."

"Doesn't feel like it."

"Come on," he said, grabbing a tray for each of us. "You know, maybe they're just staring at your super-hot-but-lacks-personality boyfriend."

I rolled my eyes. "You forgot to add 'melo-dramatic.'"

"That's good." He scratched his chin. "Maybe I should add that to the re-write."

"Add ridiculous too."

He bumped my shoulder with his. "You're mean when you're hungry."

"Then feed me."

We walked to Jon's favorite serving line—classics —which always had his staples of chicken, hamburg-ers, nachos and the like. I couldn't quite bring myself to eat there much, but I waited with him before going to the Asian grill.

They loaded my plate with grilled chicken, flavorful rice, and steamed vegetables. I couldn't wait to dig in.

When we sat down, Jon watched me take my first bites with the nervous look he always had at the beginning of a meal. Like he wanted to confirm I was following through with the nutritionist's and psychologist's advice. That I was getting better.

I didn't confront him about it because I knew his concern meant he cared. Even if the hovering bothered me. I'd done plenty to earn his worry.

"So, what's on the agenda for today?" I asked.

"I have a surprise for you."

"Yeah?"

He lifted his chin. "Actually, she's coming this way."

CHAPTER FIVE

I TWISTED in my seat to see Stormy coming toward me, looking way too adorable in a flowy polka-dot top that perfectly accentuated her growing bump.

"Stormy!" I cried, bringing even more attention to myself as I stumbled out of my chair.

She ran my way, curly hair flying behind her, and wrapped me in a hug.

"I missed you," I said, returning the embrace.

"Same, chica." She squeezed me even tighter. "Ugh. Track is stupid."

I pulled back, laughing. "So are full-time jobs."

"Right?" She flipped her hair back. "You know, other than the money."

"Money? What's that?" I laughed and looked between her and Jon. "What are you doing here?"

Her arms circled her stomach. "Mom wanted to do some shopping for the nursery."

"How long are you here?"

"We're leaving tomorrow. I was wondering if you'd want to do a girls' night at our hotel?"

"Um, duh!" I cried. Then I looked at Jon. "Sorry."

He chuckled. "I had to get some *distraction-free* studying done anyway." There was a wink in his words that Stormy caught, going by her sly smile.

"You know what distractions lead to, right?" She pointed at her stomach.

I laughed. "Come sit with us. We're almost done eating."

She and Jon shared an approving look I would have been blind to miss, but I pretended not to notice, focusing instead on my food.

Jon talked her ear off about Frank and the baby and work and life in Woodman. He needed to add kind to his list of personality traits. He could walk into a party full of strangers and have them all feeling right at home before the appetizers even arrived.

When my plate was cleared, Stormy asked, "Are you done with your homework?"

I nodded. "Finished last night, even with the *distractions*."

Jon gently kicked my leg.

"Awesome. Want to grab a bag and meet me out front?" She gave Jon and me a coy smile. "Maybe get a kiss goodbye? I know you two can't stand an hour apart from each other."

"Hey, hey, hey," Jon said. "We can stand an hour apart. It's two that's pushing it."

I giggled. "Truth."

Stormy pretended to gag herself. "Gah, I can't wait for you guys to hate each other. Just a little bit."

"Like you and Frank?" I quipped. "You're still giving each other googly eyes."

Stormy ignored my comment and stood up. "Downstairs in ten!" Then she reached onto a passerby's plate and grabbed a roll.

"What the hell?" he asked.

"I'm pregnant," she yelled back. "Sue me!"

Still laughing, Jon said, "Well, one thing's for sure. She knows how to make an exit."

"You can't miss Stormy," I agreed, then stood up. "Come on. I better get packed up."

We walked down to my dorm, and while I gathered my things for an overnight stay, he tapped on his phone screen.

"Hot date?" I asked.

He rolled his eyes. "With a D minus paper."

"Still want to tell that jerk where to shove it."

"Again with the shoving things." He shook his head, amused. "No, I'm texting Kyle. He said Anika's birthday is next Sunday. He wants some help making it special."

"That's sweet." I put the last of my toiletries into my bag and zipped it shut. I could already feel my chest tightening at the thought of being farther than a floor away from Jon. "You'll call me tonight, right?"

He held my face with both of his hands and kissed my nose. "I wouldn't miss a chance to tell you goodnight."

My heart warmed, and I closed my eyes as he kissed my forehead. "I'll see you at lunch tomorrow, okay?"

"Okay."

"Do you want me to walk you downstairs?" he asked.

"Nah," I said, trying to be brave. "I'll be fine."

Was I reassuring him or myself?

He wrapped me in a hug and held me to his chest just long enough for my heart to pace itself with the slow beats of his. "I love you, Abi Johnson."

"I love you, too, Jon Scoller."

His lips landed softly on the crown of my head. "Now, go have a good time with Stormy. She needs you."

My brows came together. "Since when did Stormy need anyone?"

"The strongest people got that way for a reason." His smile was conflicted. "I'll let her tell you herself."

CHAPTER SIX

I TURNED OVER YET another four-figure price tag and tried not to make a face.

Stormy said that was embarrassing. But gah, two thousand dollars for what equated to a baby cage on wheels? Come on.

"Is there a scratch-and-dent section?" I asked the salesperson who'd been following us around the store like we were criminals.

She pointed over her shoulder at an impossibly small yellow sign that said *sale.*

Stormy's mom grabbed her arm. "Ding, ding, ding, we have a winner."

"Cha-ching," I said.

Stormy gave us an exasperated smile. "You two are the worst," she said and followed us back to the room. Half of the fluorescent lights were burned out, casting a low, flickering hue over the room full of discarded baby gear.

Why a six-pound human needed so many things, I had no idea, but here we were in the land of lost items ready to find a home.

Stormy's mom flipped up a tag on a lamp and grinned. "That's more like it."

Stormy walked past her to a dark wooden crib and ran her hands over the surface. Her eyes gleamed, and I could tell she wasn't seeing the furniture, but her future. Her child, her world, lying on the bed.

I reached down beside her and checked the price tag. "I'm getting this for you."

Her dark, conflicted eyes found mine. "Are you sure?"

"It's the least I could do."

Her mom found a matching changing table, and Stormy picked out a rocking chair. After we paid, Stormy and her mom made plans to pick everything up the next morning before they went home.

Stormy's mom said the flickering lights had given her a headache, so we went to the hotel. They had gotten two separate rooms, and it made me even

more worried about what Stormy needed to tell me.
What was going on with my best friend?

The baby had to be okay—we'd just dropped
some serious money on the nursery—but she hadn't
mentioned Frank. My gut dropped. If he'd skipped
out, I would *end* him. Stormy and my goddaughter
deserved more than a deadbeat sperm donor.

We stood in the doorway of Stormy's mom's
room while she searched through her purse for our
room key and I made plans for revenge.

She handed one to Stormy and one to me, then
handed over the keys to her car. "Why don't you two
go have some fun while I take a nap?"

Stormy turned to me and smiled, but I had a
hard time telling whether it was real or not. "You
game?" she asked.

"Of course," I said, masking my rage.

We left the hotel, and she handed me the keys. "I
don't know why I even have these. I have no idea
where things are here."

"Me either," I admitted. "The dorm and the
track are about the extent of it. Oh, and the corn
run."

"Corn run?" she laughed.

"Yeah, it's this country loop where we go
training."

"Show me everything," she said. "I want to see what college is like."

So I obliged. We drove around campus while I told her all about my professors. The funny ones, the boring ones, the ones who always complained about teacher's pay. Then I told her about cafeteria food that all tasted the same after a while and how no one talked to each other on campus except for sorority girls who squealed at the sight of matching Comfort Colors T-shirts.

She laughed. "I bet it would be fun to join a sorority."

I rolled my eyes. "Who are you, and what have you done with my best friend?"

"Seriously," she said. "A bunch of girlfriends all living together? It would be like *Gilmore Girls,* but with frat parties and more than two cute guys at a time."

"Well, when you put it that way." I laughed.

But she was already staring out the window, her mind somewhere else.

"Let me show you the corn run," I said.

I drove out to the country roads Jon had shown me on move-in day. I confided in her about our first date at Upton, the confession he'd made. She took it all in, her eyes hungry.

"I'll never have this," she said.

"But you'll have this." I put a hand on hers that was still on top of her growing stomach. "That has to mean something."

Tears brimmed in her eyes. "Abi, I'm scared."

"Stormy, what's going on?" I pulled the car into the turn-off and waited. My heart stalled, dreading her news.

"I have pre-eclampsia, high blood pressure. It's bad for me, but it could be"—she choked on the word —"lethal for the baby." She sobbed over her lap, tears for her and Frank and the love of their lives she'd carried but not yet held.

"I think my mom got me the nursery things just to prove it would all be okay," she sniffed. "But what if it's not?"

"It will be," I said.

"Why?" she demanded, her eyes on me, desperate for answers I didn't have.

"Because it has to be," I said. "It has to be."

CHAPTER SEVEN

WE WENT BACK to the hotel room soon after her tears had run out. Stormy lay in one of the beds, flicking through TV channels, spent from her confession. I went to the bathroom and took my time, as much to relieve myself as to give her a second alone.

How could I comfort my friend when I had not the slightest idea of what she was going through? I'd never created life, been in charge of more than myself. Her worries were beyond what I could comprehend. All I knew was that I'd be there for her, no matter what happened, just like she'd been there for me.

When I walked out of the bathroom, her mouth was open and eyes closed, as she snored louder than the sitcom playing on the TV. I smiled at her, mostly because I'd finally found a pose that wasn't flattering on her. Partly because she obviously needed the sleep.

I went to her and took the remote out of her loose grip, clicked off the TV, and set the remote on the nightstand. Then I turned off all the lights except for one lamp and left the room to go on a walk around the hotel.

I'd told Stormy everything would be okay, but what if it wasn't? As I meandered toward the lobby, I searched pre-eclampsia on my phone. It sounded really scary. I wished I could reach out to my mom about this. Not my terrible mom, but the one of my dreams. One who would listen and care and know what to say to a woman scared for her health and that of her child's.

I went to the breakfast bar and made myself some green tea before sitting down at one of the tables. There were still a couple of hours before I'd normally be ready for bed, but I called Jon anyway.

He answered after the first few rings. "Hello?"

"You knew?"

There was a cringe in his answer. "Frank told me. He was worried Stormy wouldn't tell you."

My heart hurt for the girl snoring away upstairs. "Why does she think she always has to be so strong?"

"I could ask you the same thing." He paused. "How was she?"

"Scared." I slowly stirred the tea in my cup, watching the water go from clear to pale yellow. "I didn't know what to say to her, Jon."

"I don't think there's much you can say."

"What do you mean?"

"Well," he said, "it's not exactly the kind of thing you can fix. She just needs to know there will be someone there for her, no matter what."

I groaned. "It sucks watching someone hurt and not being able to do anything about it."

He snorted in response. "Tell me about it."

Well, that shut me up. He'd been there just a few months prior, watching me waste away while going through his own family tragedy.

"It's life," Jon added. "It can't be perfect."

"Why not?" I asked for Stormy just as much as for myself.

"I'll tell you when I find out."

I gave a half-hearted smile. "Gee, thanks."

"At your service."

When it became clear we couldn't solve the problems before us, we talked for a little while longer about homework and school and what we would do for Christmas break, and then we said goodbye.

After the call ended, I glanced around and realized how alone I was. There wasn't a soul to be seen in the lobby area. The receptionist was absent from the front desk. No one was trying to check in.

Suddenly, my heart raced like I was in the middle of the pasture again, and I gulped in deep breaths, trying to keep up. My therapist had told me to put my head between my knees and focus on something right in front of me. Describe every bit of it over and over until I remembered I was here. Not there.

She called it mindfulness.

I called it impossible.

I stared at the carpet underneath my feet, the rough fibers, the gray stain, the red and cream pattern, until my breathing slowed again. When I finally straightened up, I saw Stormy leaning against the wall, concern in her eyes.

"Are you okay?" she breathed.

And for whatever reason, I burst into tears, only able to shake my head before she came and held me tight, crying right along with me.

At some point, we looked up at each other, our tear-stained faces, and it hit me how far we'd come from that first day in school when she'd forced me on her motley group of friends. I reached up and held her face. "You're going to be a great mom."

She laughed and wiped at her eyes. "You mean a great mess."

"No way," I said. "Look at you. With all you're going through, you're still looking out for me and everyone else. You're going to be amazing."

"You think?" Her voice was small.

"I know."

CHAPTER EIGHT

STORMY and her mom dropped me off at the dorms the next morning, and maybe it was a good thing I was already running late for class, because saying goodbye was nearly impossible. But instead of wallowing, I hurried upstairs to grab my backpack and rushed across campus.

I kept my headphones firmly in my ears and my eyes on the sidewalk in front of me, counting the lines as I crossed them. There would be no running into anyone. No accidentally making false friends.

In my policy class, I repeated the professor's words in my mind as he said them, trying as hard as I could to stay focused on the lecture and not my fears. My past.

The images that flashed in my mind of that night were getting worse—harder to distinguish from the present. The pounding feeling in my head challenged my heart to beat faster and faster. Superseding all else was the need to glance over my shoulder and make sure Eric wasn't there.

On my way to lunch, someone tapped my back, and I screamed, ripping my earbuds out.

"Whoa," Jon said. "It's just me."

"Right." I blinked against the image of Eric reaching for me. "Right."

"Are you okay?"

"Just caught me off guard is all."

His brows came together. "Are you sure?"

I nodded. "I just..." I looked around us as we entered the dining hall. "I know it sounds crazy, but I keep seeing... It's getting worse."

Concern and understanding splashed across his face, blending in his features. "Have you talked to your counselor about it?"

"No," I said. "But I will. I have an appointment soon."

"Good." He looked like he wanted to say more, but he shook his head. "I trust you." *To get help,* he didn't say.

"Can we talk about something else?" I asked.

"Sure." He swiped in to get food. "What do you want to talk about?"

I swiped my card too and followed him to the classics line. "Something really painful. The corn run on a hundred-degree day?"

"Ha ha."

"Pap smears?"

"You're funny."

"The five minutes before a test ends and you still have a million questions left?"

"I get it, I get it. We won't talk about therapy," he said. "What about Anika's birthday? We still need to come up with some ideas to occupy her while Kyle gets her surprise ready."

"What's he planning?"

"No idea. But he's definitely not telling us," Jon said.

I raised my eyebrows. "I'm sure we can get it out of him."

"Not a chance."

"Not even if we say please?"

He laughed. "Not even if you bat those beautiful blue eyes and pout those perfect lips."

I made exactly the face he was talking about, and

ABI AND THE BOY SHE LOVES   41

he kissed away my pout, dousing my middle with warmth.

I smiled up at him. "You're kinda perfect, you know."

"Gotta take care of my girl."

"Say that again."

"That again."

Laughing, I hit his arm. "You're dumb."

"You're lovely."

A tray landed on the table next to us, and Nikki sat down in an open chair. "If you guys get any cuter, I'm going to throw up."

"Same," Mollie said, sitting down too.

Jayne shrugged before taking her seat. "I don't know; I think it's sweet."

Anika took the next spot. "Me too."

Jon looked at me. "I think we've been invaded."

The girls laughed, and Anika said, "Definitely. What have you two been talking about? Happily ever after?"

"You," Jon said flatly. "Of course."

She laughed and rolled her eyes. "Uh huh. That's what you were gazing into each other's eyes about."

I gave Jon's hand a squeeze under the table.

"So," Nikki said. "What are you two doing tonight?"

I raised my eyebrows. "Why don't you tell us?"

"Well," she said. "My dad's got a job for us to do on the farm. If you're not too chicken."

CHAPTER NINE

I DIDN'T HAVE cowboy boots, but Nikki assured me my old tennis shoes would work. Since we were in the early part of December and it had finally gotten cold in Texas, we took our own vehicles instead of getting wind-whipped in the bed of Nikki's pickup.

I sat in the front of the car with Jon while Jayne and Anika sat in the back. They'd both hit it off really well since my birthday party, and I could tell why. They were both infallibly kind. Listening to a conversation between the two of them was like watching a *Care Bear* episode for adults with boyfriends and homework.

We stopped in the yard of Nikki's family's farmhouse and got out of the car. The cold air instantly hit me, and I rubbed my gloves together, trying to warm my hands against what could easily become a bone-deep chill.

"This way," Nikki said, her breath coming out in a cloud of steam.

"What are we doing?" Anika asked.

"We've got to AI the heifers."

My brows came together. "Like artificial intelligence? Are there robot cows I don't know about?"

Anika and Nikki burst out laughing.

Okay, I knew there weren't robot cows, but seriously. I was kind of embarrassed now.

Anika said, "AI stands for artificial insemination."

"Okay, that's way worse than robot cows," I said, laughing.

Mollie laughed like she agreed.

We reached the barn where Nikki's dad was messing with a metal tank that almost looked like it could have been used for cream. But instead, the top came off and brought long, thin tubes with it.

"That's the semen," Anika explained.

"But why?" Jon asked.

She shrugged. "They put it in heifers since they're smaller, and it's easier on them than bulls."

Jon and I gave each other a look. I did not need to know this much about where my food came from.

Nikki's dad gave us a grin. "These are our helpers?"

"Yes, sir," Nikki said. "Still a little wet behind the ears, but they'll do." She gave us a conspiratorial grin.

Her dad explained the system to us, how we could get cattle through the chute while keeping them as calm as possible. And everything went well. The cows' steps sent loose dirt in the air, giving off an earthy smell. Moos sounded every so often, adding to the country feel, and I could see why people loved this. Out here, it felt like we were a part of the earth, the fundamental system of raising animals and preparing food for everyone.

I waved my arms and stepped forward to help push one of the cows along, Jon beside me doing the same thing.

But the heifer didn't want to go. She stomped at the ground, breathing hard through her nostrils, and started back at us.

"RUN!" Mollie yelled.

I split, racing toward the fence and scrambling up as fast as I could. Jon dove to the opposite side, launching through the slats and rolling on the ground outside the pen as the heifer charged back.

As I looked down over the scene, my heart thundered against my ribcage, adrenaline firing through my system like lightning. Jon stood up across the way, dusting off his jeans.

Nikki walked our way from the chute. "Everyone okay?"

"Yeah," I said, climbing down.

At the same time, Jon said, "No. Come on, Abi. We're getting out of here." He glanced at Anika and Jayne. "You two can find a ride?"

They nodded.

I looked between Jon and Nikki, my boyfriend and my best friend in college. Jon was already storming off.

I gave Nikki an apologetic look and followed Jon away from the pens and the cattle. His legs moved fast, so fast I almost had to jog to keep up with him.

"What the hell?" he said. "She took us out here to help with *that*? We have no idea what we're doing. We could have gotten hurt." He stopped at the car and waited for my response.

I couldn't understand why he was so upset. Why he'd risked offending my friends. "We were okay, though," I reminded him.

He gave me a look and got into the car.

My chest tightened as I followed suit, and his rant continued.

"Four of us are on the track team," he thundered. "At Upton on scholarship. If we get injured, that's over, Abi. No more track. No more scholarship."

I looked between him and a splinter on my hand from climbing the corral fence. "We can't just stop living our lives because we're on the track team."

"No, but we can stop taking unnecessary risks." His jaw worked as he backed out of the drive and started down the dirt road.

"I know it was scary, but we were fine," I said, laying my hand on his leg. "Nothing bad happened."

"You don't get it, do you, Abi?" he asked, then finally met my eyes. There was desperation in his gaze. A heaviness I rarely saw in him. "I'm nothing without track. Nothing."

A shard of my heart broke loose. "That's not true." *Because you'll always have me,* I wanted to say, but I couldn't bring myself to.

"It is," he asserted. "It's who I am."

CHAPTER TEN

WHEN WE GOT BACK to the dorms, I told Jon I was tired and needed to go to sleep. Mostly, I needed some time to process what had happened and find a way to apologize to Nikki.

Growing up on a ranch clearly wasn't easy. She knew that lifestyle like the back of her hand, but the hazards were all new to us. How was she supposed to know we weren't ready to run out of the way? That Jon would react so strongly to a little scare? I hadn't known myself, and we'd grown as close as two people could be.

To distract myself—mindfulness be damned—I got out my laptop and checked my emails. There were a few from professors about upcoming assignments and one from...Eleanor Dennis?

Either someone had stolen my grandma's identity or they'd taken over her mind and sent her straight to the looney bin.

I opened it up, ready for a scam email from a Nigerian Prince.

DEAR ABI,

JORGE TAUGHT ME HOW TO EMAIL. I DON'T KNOW HOWW TO TURN OFF UPPERCASE TYPING. I WILL EMAIL YOU A PACKING LIST FOR CHRISTMAS WHEN I FIGURE IT OUT. HOPE YOURE DOING WELL. LOVEE YOU TO PIECES.

GRAM

I smiled at the screen, thinking of my grandma hunting and pecking for every single letter, not being able to figure out that the light-up key on the keyboard would turn off her caps lock.

The woman was still my hero. What did that say about me?

I hit reply and typed back an email.

Dear Grandma,

That is so exciting! Tell Jorge thank you! There is a button on your keyboard that says "caps lock." Push it again and it should come off. I love you.

Abi

Within minutes, my phone lit up with a call from

Grandma. Before I even said hello, she launched in on her tirade.

"I don't know why people email when they could just call each other," she said. "Jorge said it's easier for business, but honestly, can't people just take notes? It took me fifteen minutes to type that. I could have said it in ten seconds."

I laughed. "You don't have to email me if you don't want to."

"Promise?" she said. "My friend Elise told me that's the only way she can get her grandchildren to talk to her. Takes her an hour to type out an email. I'm ashamed of how long it took me."

"No way, Gram," I said. "You can call me. Who else am I going to talk to about birth control pills?"

She laughed. "I suppose you're right."

"I am," I said.

"How's Jon doing?"

I groaned, thinking about the near miss earlier. But then I realized Grandma had known Jon even before I did. She might have some ideas of how to help. "He's...not great."

"What do you mean?"

I explained what happened—with the paper and what he'd said about running.

"Running isn't who he is," she said. "It's what he does."

"Try telling him that," I muttered.

"You know, I think it's probably tough. Being at college for running and practicing as much as you both do and getting as much praise as he does," she said. "It would be easy to get wrapped up in that and forget everything else. Winter break will be good for him. For both of you. You can remember who you are outside of college."

"I hope so," I said.

I didn't want running to be his everything. He had so much else in life. Parents who loved him, a career in social work to strive toward...me. Our future we stayed up late talking and dreaming about.

"It'll be okay," Grandma said like she could hear my thoughts. "Honey, I have to go. Jorge just finished cooking dinner."

"You know what comes after dinner, young lady?" I said in my best "mom" voice.

"Dessert?"

I laughed at the false innocence in her tone. "Enjoy."

"Goodnight, sweetie."

Without the distraction of my grandma, I texted

Nikki an apology and then threw myself into planning Anika's birthday. Running might have been Jon's life, but my loved ones were mine. I wanted them to know that.

CHAPTER ELEVEN

AROUND THREE IN the morning of Anika's birthday, I woke up to my phone alarm. She was typically a pretty heavy sleeper, but I'd set it to vibrate, just in case. Thankfully, she was still asleep.

I crept to my desk and got rolls of crepe paper and tape from the bottom drawer. In my best ninja moves ever, I covered our room in the stuff, wrapping it around the ladder to her loft bed, her desk chair, the rod in her closet, over her shoes.

When my eyes had fully adjusted to the dark and I was sure the room looked thoroughly—and ridiculously—festive, I climbed back into my bed and fell asleep again.

I woke up to Anika's squeal with light pouring

through the windows and drool running down my cheek.

"Oh my gosh, Abi!" she yelled. "You did this?"

I wiped at my cheek and pushed myself up. In the morning light, my crepe job looked way shabbier, but the way Anika was grinning, it had gotten my point across. Just in case, I said, "Happy birthday, roomie!"

"Thank you." She fingered a loose end of crepe paper hanging on her guard rail and shook her head. "You're crazy."

I laughed. "That's kind of the point. Now, get showered up because I'm taking you out."

She glanced at her phone. "At nine in the morning? There're just creeps and drunks at the bar this time of day."

I shrugged, then shooed her toward the door, knowing what was coming next. "Go."

"You're bossy." She climbed down her ladder, paper ripping on her way down.

"You're slow," I said. "Shoo."

Still shaking her head, she grabbed an outfit and her shower caddy and headed toward the door. The second she opened it, balloons and streamers cascaded over her, just like Kyle, Jon, and I had planned.

Covered in glitter, she turned to me and blew some off her lips. "I take back my comment about crazy. You're certifiable."

"I take that as a compliment."

She laughed. "I'll be back in fifteen."

While she changed and showered, I grabbed a pair of shorts, a T-shirt, and tennis shoes for her out of her dresser, then put them in a big purse. I put on sweats and left my workout clothes on underneath. By the time she came back, I was ready to go.

We drove in my car across town, and I parked in front of the restaurant.

"When you said we were going out, I hadn't planned for breakfast." She laughed.

I shrugged. "Pancakes are my idea of pregaming."

We went inside and sat together at a booth. While we waited for the waitress to take our order, I made conversation. "Do you know what Kyle has planned for later?"

"No idea," she said behind her menu. "And he refuses to budge."

"I know," I grumbled. "I tried to get him to tell me the other night, and he was adamant."

She rolled her eyes, but in that way that said she

kind of admired his determination. "I just need to be patient."

"You are a stronger woman than I." I set my own menu on the table. "Do you have any guesses? He's not proposing, is he?"

"No way," she said. "My parents would die."

I raised my eyebrows. "You're nineteen. It's not like you're a child."

"Yeah, but they don't want me to drop out of college or lose focus. Or get pregnant."

My heart hurt for Stormy just then. I knew Anika hadn't meant to, but she'd just insinuated getting pregnant would be an end to her options. It wasn't. It couldn't be.

"So what else?" I asked. "I know he's not planning a sexcapade or anything like that."

Her cheeks heated. "Knowing Kyle, it's probably something super sweet and heartfelt."

"Well, I feel like a jerk."

"Don't," she said. "Even if you were, I'd let you off for insanity. I'm pretty sure I'll never get the glitter out of my hair."

I laughed. "I knew the streamers were a good idea."

The waitress came back, and we ordered and ate breakfast together, just talking and catching up about school and our boyfriends and our friends back home.

She told me she used to have a pen pal, and her friends conspired to help her see him at outside of school, even though her parents would have died before letting her do something like that. Just one way her friends had backed her up.

"I miss Bran and Leslie so much," she said. "We try to stay in touch, but it's hard with being at different schools, you know?"

I fought to keep my face normal. "When will you see them next?"

She pouted. "Not until Christmas. Ugh."

The waitress brought our check, and I paid for it.

"Where to next?" she asked.

"You'll see."

We drove back across town to the campus, and I parked in a metered spot in front of the rec center. Usually, I'd make her walk forever with me, but it was my girl's birthday. And I couldn't wait to show her the surprises waiting for her inside.

"What are we doing here?" she asked.

I started toward the doors. "I heard you loved volleyball?"

She nodded.

"Well..." I reached into my purse and handed her

the clothes. "Go change, then meet us in the gym. We've got a pick-up game planed."

We got through the doors and swiped into the building. I'd been here a few times, mostly just exploring. Enough to know where we were going.

Once she was on her way to the women's locker room, I hurried to the gym. I hoped everyone had shown up on time as planned.

A group of people sprawled around the gym floor, stretching, hanging out. I recognized Jon, Kyle, some girls from the track team, and then two other people from the photos on Anika's board.

They stood with Kyle and Jon, talking, laughing.

"Hey," I said, joining them.

Kyle's eyes lit up. "Where's our girl?"

"Changing." I looked at Bran and Leslie. "She's going to be so excited to see you two."

Leslie rubbed her hands together, her eyes giving away just how much she wanted to see her best friend. "Let's hope that makes up for how terrible Bran is at volleyball."

"Hey," he said. "It's not my fault Mr. Mullen ran in front of me while I was serving."

"He was behind you," Leslie said, laughing.

"Minor details."

Anika's shrieked from behind me. "WHAT?!"

She ran into the gym and attacked her friends, wrapping them in a hug.

Bran looked over her shoulder and winked at Kyle. "Told you she loved me more."

I smiled at them. They made me miss my friends even more.

"Come on, come on," Kyle said, pretending to be annoyed. "We've got a game to play."

For the next couple of hours, we scrimmaged. I wasn't very good, but at least I was better than Bran. To be fair, it wasn't hard to outplay him. He hit the thirty-foot ceiling twice on wild passes, somehow rolled over the top of the ball while trying to pick it up, and his serves made me wonder if he thought we were playing dodgeball instead of volleyball. But he was hilarious. I could see why Anika liked him so much and had pictures of him all over her corkboard.

As we broke for lunchtime, Leslie put her arm around Anika's shoulders and said to the rest of us, "Okay, I think Bran and I can take it from here."

While our friends filtered out of the gym, I turned to Jon and said, "What now?"

He gave me a sultry look and crooked his finger. "Follow me. I have an idea."

CHAPTER TWELVE

HE LED me to one of the lower levels of the rec center, past an abandoned badminton court.

"There's no one down here," I said.

"That's kind of the point," he replied. He stopped at a door labeled Men's Locker Room and took me inside.

"Wait here," he said.

He disappeared around a corner, and I stood in the doorway for a few moments wondering what he had planned for me down here.

When he came back, missing his shirt, he said, "All clear."

My heart started racing for entirely different reasons. Jon wasn't thinking what I was thinking...was he?

"Come on." He took my hand and led me farther back, past maroon lockers and old shower stalls until we were standing in front of a wooden hut. A sauna. "Want to fog up the windows with me?"

I hit his shoulder. "You're ridiculous."

"That's why you love me." He grabbed a couple towels from the stack and handed me one.

I took it from him, then slipped off my shoes and followed him inside. It hadn't completely warmed up yet, but sweat still sprang to the surface of my skin. Jon sat on the opposite side of the sauna and said, "Give me your foot."

"A foot rub?" I asked. "Now I know you're the one."

He rolled his eyes. "Hand it over."

"Don't you mean foot it over?"

"That was lame."

"And?"

He nodded toward my foot.

I lifted it, and he took it in his hands, slowly rubbing all the knots and callouses that came from being on the track team. His rhythmic touch felt like...heaven.

"Just a couple weeks until winter break," he said.

"I know. I can't wait. Grandma already emailed me my packing list."

He raised his eyebrows. "Your grandma can email?"

"Jorge showed her," I explained, a smile finding my lips. "He just didn't show her how to turn off the caps lock."

He laughed. "Did you get some shouty emails?"

"Just one. And a frustrated phone call."

Still smiling, he closed his eyes and leaned his head back. "I can't wait to show you the cabin."

"Do you think we'll get our own room?" I asked.

"With my parents? Not a chance. I can't believe I'm saying this, but they're not as progressive as your grandma."

I laughed. "You mean the woman who just got her very first laptop?"

"That's the one."

"I can't wait to try snowboarding."

"Are you sure?" he asked. "I wouldn't want you getting hurt."

How could I get it through to him? I wasn't worried about a sprained ankle or even a more serious injury if it meant living life to its fullest. "I want to try everything," I said. "After...what happened, I don't want to let life pass me by playing it safe. This might be the only chance I get to try it."

"Don't think like that," he said. "We have plenty

of time for you to try snowboarding, skiing...heck, even tubing."

"But I have to try it now," I said. "You don't understand. When I was running away from Eric, there was a very real chance I wouldn't have made it through the night. If he wouldn't have wrecked..." I cringed against the image of his pickup sideways in the gully and his headlights flooding the countryside. "If he had hit me with his gunshots, I wouldn't be here with you now. I don't want to waste a minute."

"Then we won't." He set my foot down and came to sit next to me. His lips captured mine in a salty kiss that showed me just how much he meant it.

CHAPTER THIRTEEN

UNFORTUNATELY, our rendezvous in the sauna was the last chance we really had to spend any significant amount of time alone together for the last few weeks of the semester.

Finals demanded our full attention, along with our track coaches who were trying to get us in the best shape possible before winter break came along and set us back.

The rest of the students at Upton would have nearly a full month off of school, but the track team got two weeks. Still, that two weeks could easily derail months of progress if we weren't careful.

Jon and I studied together, ate together, and walked to practice together on the rare occasion our schedules lined up, but that was about it.

Although it seemed like I'd just started college a week prior, I found myself on the Friday before semester break about to take my last final. I sat in the study lounge nearest my political science classroom, poring over my notes for some last-minute cramming. A TV played in the lounge, permanently set to a local news station.

Stories about winter storms and upcoming Christmas events played in the background, making me feel almost like I was at home with Grandma, working on homework while she watched her nightly news.

"Eric Shepherd, the culprit in an attempted murder nearly two months ago, is being released from the hospital today, into police custody."

My body strummed tight like a wire ready to break, and my neck snapped back to look at the TV. There was his face on the screen. Eric.

He looked battered still, hair shaved close to reveal long lines of stitches on his head as he walked away from the hospital, handcuffed and escorted by police officers. The news cameras did a close-up on his face. He was unrecognizable. Except for his eyes. The blank stare there attacked my soul. They were dead, just like they had been *that* night.

"He will stay in county jail without bail until a court date is set."

Just like that, the anchor flipped to another story like a monster hadn't just been on the screen. Like that simple piece of information hadn't sent me spiraling back to running so hard my shoes burned through my feet. To the memory of some stranger ripping cactus spines out of my skin. To gunshots firing behind me.

The bell tower rang on the hour, making me jump about a million and a half miles out of my skin. My notes went flying to the floor.

Someone nearby, a girl I recognized from class, helped me pick them up. I barely managed a "thank you."

She held out the notes. "Are you okay? You look like you're about to pass out."

I shook my head and said, "I'm fine," being sure to take several deep breaths, just in case.

Tears brimmed in my eyes. Why me? Why now? I was moments from taking one of the most important tests for me to get into law school, and I could hardly put one foot in front of the other, much less remember the results of Gideon v. Wainwright.

I didn't have time to go back and collect myself—call my therapist for an emergency session. Our professor had made it very clear that if anyone was late, they wouldn't be allowed to take the final.

So, I walked into the classroom, head down, and sat in the front row. I put my notes in front of me, and I read the words over and over again, trying to remind myself that I was here, not there.

But then Professor Beauford's TA was passing out the tests, telling us to put our notes away and keep our eyes on our own papers.

I worked through each question, but my mind couldn't focus. I wound up selecting the third answer on each one and left the room with tears threatening to fall.

"Miss Johnson," the professor called behind me.

I turned to him but kept my face down, trying to hide the emotions spilling over my eyelashes.

"Let's step outside," he said, then hurried an order to his TA.

I followed him into the gloriously empty hallway.

"What's going on?" he asked, his lined face showing more emotion than it had all semester.

I looked toward the sky, tried to hold in all the tears. "He's—Eric—he's out of the hospital."

He folded his arms and covered his mouth with his hand. "When did you find out?"

"They played it on the news," I said flatly. "Right before I walked into the classroom."

He put a hand on my shoulder in the kindest gesture I'd seen from him all semester. "You worry about you right now."

I nodded, but as I walked away, I still didn't know what that meant. Had I failed my first semester of college?

CHAPTER FOURTEEN

ON MY WAY back to the dorms, I tried calling my therapist's office, but since it was part of the university, it had already closed for winter break. The entire campus around me looked empty. There were actually parking spots up close. The sidewalks were atypically sparse, and there was a chill in the air that seemed to silence everything.

That only made the pounding in my head and heart seem that much louder.

I dialed Jon's number and held the phone to my ear with both hands.

When he answered, I finally felt like I could breathe. "Jon."

"How was the test?"

"Horrible," I cried, my voice shaking. "Eric is out of the hospital!"

There was a pause. His voice was harsh as he uttered, "What?"

"I saw it on the news, Jon, right before I went in for the test."

"Wasn't the police department supposed to call you?"

"Before his trial," I said, my whole body shaking now. "They haven't set the date. Yet."

"Are you okay?"

I laughed. Kind of. More like a hysterical sound that seemed at odds with the quiet world around me. "No, I'm not okay."

"Where are you?"

"Almost to the dorms."

"I'll be there. Put me on video call."

I stopped in the middle of the sidewalk and did as he asked. He was throwing on a hoodie, yanking on his shoes.

I held one hand over my pounding heart. The heart that was his. "Hurry," I breathed.

"I am." He passed the elevator altogether and flew down the stairs, all the way from the ninth floor. His breathing came so fast he couldn't talk, but words weren't necessary.

This was Jon, and he was coming.

The lobby passed behind him on the screen, and when he got to the front door of the dorms, I saw him. I wanted to run to him, but my legs wouldn't move. I couldn't think. Everything was starting to sound far away.

I focused on Jon. On his face. On the fact that he was here. I was here.

He wrapped me in his arms, and I breathed him in. If I was holding on to him, I couldn't get lost in the depths of my mind. Right now, it was a pretty scary place. I just hoped I could get out.

Jon led me to his dorm room, his arm holding me up the entire way. He seemed to be the only thing in my world that wasn't constantly shaking and swaying.

Inside his room, he guided me to his bed, helped me up, and then lay beside me, cocooning my shivering body with his warm one. "I'm right here," he whispered. "You're safe." Over and over again, he whispered those two powerful words until I finally let exhaustion carry me to sleep.

When I woke up, Jon still had his arms around me. He brushed my hair away from my face. "How are you feeling, beautiful?"

"Better," I said. The shock of the news about Eric

had worn off, and all I was left with was a dull thud in my brain that reminded me of what I had been though.

He let out a relieved breath and kissed my forehead. "Good."

I closed my eyes, wanting to feel every second of his touch.

"We're going to have a good break," he said in a soothing voice. "We'll get home, see our friends, be with family. And we have five whole days at Red River. It'll be us, the slopes, hot chocolate. You're going to love it there."

I knew I would. Just because he was there. Still, I needed to get out of Austin. Out of this place where fantasy had quickly turned into a nightmare.

"Let's go home?" I begged.

"Yes. I'm driving."

We were going to take both of our cars home, but I didn't mind leaving mine here. I wouldn't be going anywhere without Jon anyway.

"I just need to get my bags," I said. "They're already packed."

"Hold on." He got his phone out, sending a text. "One of the guys on the team will come help."

"Are you sure?"

"Yeah, already asked. Just need to tell them that we're ready."

I smiled up at him. "And you said you didn't have any friends."

"Enough about me," he said. "Let's get you home."

We couldn't get there soon enough.

CHAPTER FIFTEEN

MARTA TREATED us to a homecoming feast. Food just like from my first dinner there covered the table, bringing with it the most delicious smells. This topped the classics line every. Single. Time.

There was an extra place setting at the table now that Jorge had become a fixture. From the way Grandma looked at him—and he at her—he wouldn't be going anywhere anytime soon.

We usually didn't pray at the table, but Marta insisted on blessing the food this time.

I folded my hands in front of me and peeked under my lashes at the others who had their heads bowed and eyes closed.

Okay, maybe I should stop being a creep and close my eyes too.

"Dear God," Marta said. "Thank you for bringing our children home safe and sound. Thank you for giving them a successful first semester of college, in running and academics, and thank you for the wonderful people around this table. Amen."

When I opened my eyes, Marta's were shining. It made me realize we'd all been through a lot. They'd said goodbye to their only child. Had nearly lost me. But we'd all come out on the other side of it, together.

"So, what's the agenda for tomorrow?" Grandma asked.

Glen pulled a folded piece of paper from his back pocket. "Glad you asked." He slid his glasses down his nose and read each item on the itinerary. Including a six in the morning departure.

At our facial expressions, he said, "Don't worry. You'll have plenty of chances to sleep in while we're there."

Good. Getting up that early was for the birds. I knew because I'd been doing it all semester for track practice. I needed a break.

"Did we decide which cars we're taking?" Grandma asked.

Glen tucked the paper back into his pocket. "We can take ours and Jon's. I figured the lovebirds —the younger ones—would want to share some time together and the four of us can take the SUV."

"Perfect," Grandma said.

Conversation stalled as we dished up our food and got lost in how good it was. Or maybe that was just me. Because I couldn't speak through the heaven in my mouth. I needed to be careful or I would be right back to overeating and relying on food for comfort.

When Jon cleared his plate, he said, "If it's alright with you, Abi and I are going to see our friends before we have to leave tomorrow."

Our friends. My heart warmed.

"Of course," Marta said. "We'll get the dishes."

Grandma looked at me. "Will you be back tonight?"

I nodded. "Don't wait up, though."

We escaped to the car, and the second we got in, Jon fired it up. I flipped the heater to full blast, and he gave me an exasperated eye-roll.

"You knew this about me," I said, buckling in.

"I know, I know." He mimicked my voice. "'I don't want to waste any hot air.'"

"To be fair"—I nudged him—"there's plenty coming from you."

"Hardy har har." He put the car in gear and started toward Stormy's house.

"Who all's going to be there?" I asked.

"When I talked to Frank, he said the whole crew should be there."

"You and Frank are talking a lot," I commented.

He shrugged. "I think we have more in common than I originally thought."

I didn't ask what he thought they had in common. I was just glad he had someone to go to.

"Oh," I said, "I forgot to ask. How did your rewrite go?"

"Rewrite?"

"Of the personality assignment. From that as—"

"Professor?" he finished. "Don't ask."

"That bad?"

"Well, if you're ready to shove that D somewhere…"

I raised my eyebrows. "You still got a D?"

"Yep," he said flatly. "D plus, actually. So let's talk about something else."

"We can listen to music," I suggested, and at his nod, I turned up the radio. It didn't matter what was playing. Jon clearly wasn't in the mood to talk, and I understood. I just didn't understand his professor. I wanted to read the paper, but that seemed as realistic right now as Grandma having a love child with Jorge and eloping to Mexico. Although, that would make for some great awkward family photos...

We arrived at Stormy's, and after we all greeted each other, she pulled the girls into the nursery to show us around.

My heart melted at the sweet set-up. There was the crib I'd bought for her, soft gray starry decorations, and a large framed quote hanging above the crib. *You are my sun, my moon, and all of my stars. EE Cummings.*

"It's beautiful," Skye breathed.

I nodded in agreement, speechless.

Macy held Stormy in a side-armed hug. "Your baby is so lucky to have you."

Stormy circled her stomach in a protective way. I wondered if the others knew about her pre-eclampsia. Had she told them? Had Frank?

Stormy settled into the rocking chair. "Well, I did want to show you all, but honestly, I need some girl time. Frank is driving me nuts."

I sat down on the chevron rug and rested my back against the crib. "What's going on?"

Skye dropped down beside me, and Macy and Leanne leaned against the opposite wall. With Stormy in the chair, it almost looked like story time.

She rolled her eyes and pulled her legs up to sit cross-legged. "I can't believe I'm saying this, but it's almost like he's too nice. He won't let me do anything for myself!"

I laughed. "Shouldn't you be happy someone's getting you pickles and ice cream?"

Skye nudged me. "That's just a myth. My sister only wanted cheese enchiladas."

"Oh no," Stormy said. "I want it all. Everything. I'm like a vacuum cleaner." She made a sucking sound, and I laughed.

Leanne chuckled. "Isn't that what got you pregnant?"

Macy giggled with her.

Stormy pretended to be mad. "Take an anatomy lesson. That's the safe way."

I pretended to gag myself.

Skye's cheeks got red.

"New subject," Macy said. "Where's Michele? Parents wouldn't let her out?"

Stormy cringed. "I don't think things are going so well between her and Freckles."

I leaned forward. "What?"

Stormy shrugged. "I think she's being too possessive and he's getting tired of it."

Leanne raised her eyebrows. "I thought he wasn't fazed by anything."

Stormy turned up one corner of her mouth. "Guess she found his button."

Macy cracked up laughing.

Stormy grabbed a pillow and threw it at her. "You have exactly five months to grow up." Then her expression sobered. "At least, I do."

CHAPTER SIXTEEN

I'D MEANT to talk to Jon on the way to Red River, but mostly, I slept. Whether it was the early hour, staying out the night before, or the warm air blowing over my face, I couldn't keep my eyes open. When I finally woke up, we were driving through a grassy basin, mountains rising on all sides of us.

I adjusted my seat up and stared out the window to get a better look. "It's beautiful."

"I know," Jon said. "I love it here."

I grinned over at him, drinking in his beautiful green eyes as they took in the landscape. I allowed myself to imagine us, years in the future, going on a trip to the mountains with our own children. I wanted this to be a tradition we kept forever.

The road narrowed as we got closer to the mountain and began the winding path to the top. Signs for Red River passed, along with miles and miles of forest and snow.

"They've been getting tons of snow this winter," Jon said. "Should be a good time to learn. If you're still insisting on it."

I gave him a sideways look. "I'm not insisting. I'm going to."

He barely bit back a smile, instead pretending to be exasperated. "But when we get there, Mom and Dad are going to go to their favorite place to eat. Eleanor and Jorge will go with them. We're going to say we're too tired."

"But I just slept for, like, five hours."

"We're going to say we're too tired." He raised his eyebrows and gave me an exaggerated wink.

"Ah." My cheeks reddened as I caught his drift. "Now that you mention it, I am feeling sleepy." I let out a fake yawn.

"That's the spirit."

He reached over and held my hand. "Really, I'm excited to spend some time just the two of us. No responsibilities."

"It's long overdue," I agreed.

He followed his parents' car into the driveway of

a large cabin with expansive glass windows facing the mountains.

I stared at it, open-mouthed. "What happened to the bed/shower test?" I started singing their jingle. It was still burned into my brain from state cross-country all those months ago.

He chuckled as he put his car into park. "This is the one time a year we splurge."

As we got out, I stuck my hands in my pockets to guard them from the wind. The sun was shining, though, even with all the snow. It was nice.

Marta stood in front of the cabin and spread her arms. "This is it."

Glen walked toward the front door and reached into the mailbox, retrieving a set of keys. "Let us show you around."

They gave us a tour of the cabin, complete with large-screen televisions, wide beds with pine frames, and an already crackling fireplace.

"Is this heaven?" I asked.

Glen laughed. "Pretty close. Elevation nine thousand feet."

Marta nodded. "So, that means we all need to drink water, get plenty of rest, and eat some good food."

"Exactly," Glen agreed. "So, first on the agenda,

T Bucks. They have the best food in town, and they even have a fireplace in the middle of the restaurant."

It sounded great, but I made my best bleary eyes and said, "I'm so tired. Would it be alright if I passed?"

"Me too," Jon said, yawning very convincingly. "She slept most of the way, and I didn't get a break."

"You could have stopped to take a break." Marta looked concerned. "Want us to bring you something back?"

"Nah," Jon said. "I'll take her to T Bucks after we get a little rest."

They agreed to leave, on the condition we both drank a bottle of water before going to our *separate* rooms.

After they walked out the door, Jon gave me an evil grin. "Your place or mine?"

CHAPTER SEVENTEEN

"BREAKFAST IS READY!" Marta called from the kitchen.

I blinked my eyes open groggily, but the smell of eggs and meat perked me right up. Still, I grabbed my toiletries to freshen up before going to the kitchen. I opened my bedroom door and walked right into Jon. The air carried a chill, but his body was warm, covered in sweatpants and a hoodie, the socks I bought him for Christmas the year before.

"I like your socks," I said.

He wrapped his arms around my waist, pulling me closer. "I like you."

I covered my mouth with one of my hands. "You'll like me less when you smell my morning breath."

He lowered his voice and pulled my hand away. "You act like I haven't smelled it while you were snoring away."

My cheeks flushed, and I looked down, but he lifted my chin up and pressed the lightest of kisses to my lips. "That's better," he mumbled.

I smiled against his kiss. "It is a nice way to wake up. Breakfast and kisses."

"Come on," he said, taking my hand. "Let's grab some grub."

I held up my bag of toiletries. "Just because you don't care how bad I smell doesn't mean the others won't."

Smiling, he shook his head. "See you out there."

I watched him walk away for longer than I should have before continuing to the bathroom. With the door shut behind me and Jon's...assets out of sight, I realized this was probably the one place in the cabin that wasn't completely updated, with a pink shell sink and brass fixtures.

I kind of felt more at home in this bathroom.

What did that say about me?

I decided not to think about it and went about brushing my teeth and washing my face, then tying my hair back in a set of braids. I wanted to look cute snowboarding. Snowy kisses and pictures were a must.

When I walked out to the kitchen, everyone was seated at the dining room table—it actually had more than enough room for everyone. Glen was in the early stages of a massive jigsaw puzzle, while Jorge worked on a weathered crossword book and Grandma and Marta eyed a map of the town, sipping coffee with steam pouring off the brown liquid.

And then there was Jon. Stuffing his face with a breakfast burrito like he didn't have a care in the world.

I let out a giggle, to which he said, "What?" through a mouth full of food.

Marta shook her head, feigning disappointment. "You have no shame."

He gulped down his bite. "Shame? What's that?"

Laughing, I took a burrito of my own, poured myself a mug of coffee, and sat down beside Jon. All this cold weather with the winter sun streaming through the windows just made me want to cuddle, but we had an adventure to get to.

"When do you want to hit the slopes?" I asked.

"'Hit the slopes?'" Jon said. "You sound so official."

I used my coffee mug as a mask to hide my embarrassment. "I might have read a blog or two."

"Yeah?"

"Watched a few YouTube videos."

"Uh huh."

"Read a manual." I set my cup down. "You know, the basics."

Grandma lifted her cup in a salute. "That's my girl."

"You mean *my* girl," Jon teased.

Grandma winked at him. "Not until you're married."

I nearly choked on my drink. I could have choked a second time because no one chimed in to shut down the idea. They just went about their breakfast like the idea of Jon and me being married was perfectly normal. Compatible with reality.

"Deal," Jon said. Apparently he was in on the conspiracy.

I must have looked at him like he had a second head, because he said, "What? It's not like I can fight her about it."

I wiped my expression. Or tried to, at least. "That's not it."

Glen scrubbed his chin. "Nine letter word for something they need to get first? Anyone?"

Jorge lifted a finger. "Education!"

There it was. Finally.

"We get it," Jon said, sounding more disgruntled than playful. He turned to me. "You about ready?"

"Yep." I took a final bite of my burrito and a few more sips of my coffee on the way to the sink.

Grandma looked up at us. "You two be safe out there. And wear a helmet. Both of you. There was a story in the news two nights ago of a kid who—"

"I know, I know," I rushed out, not needing to hear the gory details. "We'll wear helmets."

"Speak for yourself," Jon muttered.

Grandma gave him her trademark stare down.

Like she'd worked some kind of Jedi magic on him, Jon said, "We'll wear helmets."

"Good boy," she said.

Marta added, "Abi, I put all of your snow gear in a bag by the door! You should both be set."

"Thanks," I said. "I can't believe you got all that for me."

Glen gave a small nod toward Jorge. "We might have had a little help."

My mouth slackened. Retired Jorge had bought me brand-name winter gear without saying anything? I wanted to hug him, but...we weren't at the hugging stage yet. We were barely past the awkward-greeting-because-you're-dating-my-grandma stage.

"Thank you." I tried to put all the feeling I could into the phrase.

Jorge carefully lettered in his crossword puzzle. "Nine letters, two words for you're welcome."

I thought about it for a second. "No problem."

He looked up at me and winked. "Exactly, kid."

I smiled. "Really, thank you."

"Your grandmother would kill me if we let you get frostbitten."

"Please." Grandma batted him with her hand. She looked like a silly schoolgirl. In love.

Why did it put a dopey smile on my face?

Jon took my hand. "Let's go."

I followed him out the door, ready to get back into our very own love story.

CHAPTER EIGHTEEN

HE DROVE over the slippery roads to a ski rental place—the Sitzmark. They fitted me for a snow-board, asking all sorts of questions about my height and weight and whether I was "goofy" or not.

Jon said of course I was, and I hit him before I even knew what it meant.

Good thing he was wearing a helmet.

We walked out of the shop, walking "goofy" in our snowboard boots that felt more like wooden clogs rising halfway up our calves.

"How do people walk in these?" I asked.

"They don't," Jon said. "You're supposed to ride, bruh."

I rolled my eyes. "Now who's been reading too many blogs?"

Ignoring my question, he flipped a braid over my shoulder. "That's a tubular look."

There wasn't even enough space in my head for this level of eye-roll. "I'm pretty sure that's a surfing term."

He shrugged. "Slope-ular, dude."

"Don't call me dude."

We stopped by the car, and before I could open my door, he boxed me in, his breath turning to steam in front of my face. Suddenly my blood was running hot in the cold air.

"What should I call you?" he asked low.

I lifted my chin, meeting his eyes. "Yours."

"I like the sound of that." He kissed me slow, hard, saying a million words in the span of a few seconds, each reminding me how much I really was his. There would never be anyone else. Especially not if he kept kissing me like this.

Someone nearby cleared their throat. When I looked to the side, I saw a guy jerk his head toward his kids.

Jon gave me another kiss, then whispered, "They should see what love looks like."

For me, it looked like his green eyes sparkling in the light reflecting from the snow.

He squeezed my arms, then opened the door for

me and walked/swaggered/swayed to his side of the car. If the lifts weren't so close, I would worry more about how he was going to drive in those things.

Somehow, he managed, and we got there alive. To be fair, we were only going about twenty miles an hour, so the worst that could have happened was a ding or two. We got out of the car, and Jon grabbed both of our boards. Everyone around us was walking the same silly way, talking excitedly to each other. I'd always dreamed of a beach vacation, but I was starting to like the vibe I got here.

Jon went inside the lodge to grab our lift tickets, and I stared at the lifts carrying people up the mountain, boards and skis dangling from their legs as they got farther and farther away.

"Maybe by the end of the day you'll be ready for that," Jon said.

I looked at him, and he held out a ticket and a zip tie.

"Stick it through your zipper," he instructed.

I waggled my eyebrows. "What did you say about sticking it?"

"You're ridiculous."

"Hey, that's my line," I said, fiddling with the zip tie.

"Yeah, yeah," he replied.

Once I got the tie secured, Jon covered my hands with his and zipped my coat all the way up to my chin.

"You're so cute," he said, his eyes shining.

I couldn't help but smile up at him. "It's the helmet, right?"

"Oh yeah." He knocked on it. "It doesn't make you look dorky at all."

"I'll be sure to tell Grandma thanks."

"Good."

"Good."

"Great."

He chuckled. "Come on. Let's get started."

* * *

"Is it this humanly possible to fall on your butt so many times?" I whined.

Jon gracefully dropped to his knees. "I mean, it shouldn't be."

I glared at him, then realized I had mirrored goggles on. So I stuck my tongue out instead.

"Here's what you do," he said, popping back up. "Instead of looking at the ground like this, lift your chin. If you look down, you're going to fall."

"But how will I know where I'm going?"

He pointed at one of the little kids whizzing by us on a snowboard—the show-off. "See how he has his arm out in front of him? He's following his fingers."

I watched him slide to the bottom of the bunny slope and make the perfect stop before unlatching himself from the board.

"Okay, I'll try," I said. "But there better be some hot cocoa and a back rub waiting for me when we get home."

"Sure," Jon said. "I'm sure your gram will help you out."

This time, I raised my shades so he could get the full glare-y effect.

He tossed his head back and laughed, his pink cheeks looking even brighter. "Get going. Unless you're chicken."

"If I was a chicken, I'd fly down the hill," I grumbled.

"But you're not. So chop-chop."

I flipped my goggles back down and edged myself up to standing. My board began slipping underneath me, and my stomach bottomed out in a bout of pre-fall adrenaline. But this time, I looked up. I bent my knees and pointed. And then I slid down the hill—on purpose, in control.

Jon whooped behind me, and I tried to focus on the task in front me instead of who was watching, just like we were at a track meet.

I nearly wiped out a couple of times, but before long, I was at the bottom of the hill, cheering, forgetting I was strapped to the board and jumping up and down.

And then I fell.

Jon slid to a stop next to me, laughing harder than I'd heard him laugh in a long time. Eventually, I forgot to be embarrassed and laughed right along with him.

"You know what this means?" Jon asked, still smiling.

"What?" I asked.

He pointed a gloved hand at the big lift. "It means you're ready."

CHAPTER NINETEEN

THE LIFT SWEPT us off our feet and carried us up the mountain. I clung to the handle, watching the snowy ground pass below us. Countless people made fast lines and lazy curves down the slope.

The farther we got from the bottom, the quieter it got, chatter getting replaced by wind and the whirring of the lift.

"What do you think?" Jon asked.

I smiled over at him. "I think this is what making the most of every moment looks like."

He reached over and squeezed my hand. Even with layers of gloves between us, the gesture sent warmth radiating up my arm. "Good."

For the rest of the ride, I turned my gaze back toward the passing trees and scenery, but the closer we got to the top, the more my heart began to race. "What if I fall?" I asked.

"Keep your board pointed forward and crawl out of the way."

"That's it?"

"They've seen it all," he reassured. "If they need to, they can stop the lift."

That made me feel a little bit better. At least instead of getting mowed over by a strip of wood, I'd be humiliated in front of people who actually knew what they were doing. Yay, me.

"Lift the toe of your board," Jon instructed.

The lift crested the mountain.

"Get your footing," he said.

I stood on the board.

"And go!"

I took off down the small slope and immediately lost my balance. My arms flung out wildly, and I grabbed on to the only thing I could reach.

Jon.

We both crashed to the ground, and he yelled, "Abi! How about a warning?"

"Sorry!" I cried, scooting toward the edge of the path like he'd told me. "I was scared!"

He made it to the side, flipped over, and started

brushing off his arms. "It's okay. Just means you'll be getting payback later."

"What are you going to do? Make me fall?" I snorted. "I don't mean to brag, but I've been doing a pretty good job of that on my own."

"True." He laughed and popped back up.

I did the same, only not as gracefully, and followed him to the top of the run. From here, we could see everything. The basin we'd driven through the day before, the beginning of the trail down the mountain, the lodge, the pretty little town of Red River. "Wow," I breathed.

"It's amazing," Jon said. "Just took eleven thousand feet to see it."

"That's how high up we are?"

"Yep," he said and took in a deep breath. "Two thousand feet to go to get back to the bottom."

When he put it like that, this seemed like a much worse idea. I could only imagine how much falling I could accomplish in two thousand feet. "Don't remind me."

"You can do it," he said. "Remember when you first started running? You weren't Upton-ready right away. We'll take it nice and slow. Just tell me when you need a break."

That was true. Why was I expecting myself to be

amazing at snowboarding after only a few hours of practice? I needed to cut myself some slack.

"Okay, I'm ready," I said. I nudged the toe of my board forward and began to make my own way. I'd done it before, and I could do it now.

I wiped out. Once, twice, three times. My thighs burned only a little bit more than my lungs. But I lived for those moments when the wind was rushing past me and little flecks of snow hit my goggles and melted away. This was what freedom and power and capability felt like. It was even better knowing Jon was right behind me.

After a particularly spectacular crash, I scooted to the edge of the trail and flopped back on a pile of snow left behind by the grooming machines.

"Tired?" Jon asked, moving toward me.

"Extremely."

"I think we're about halfway down."

"Save yourself," I said. "Leave me here."

"Never." He flopped down beside me, lacing his hands behind his head.

I pushed my goggles back on my helmet and turned my head toward him. Something about the snow and the gray sky made him look even more attractive. And I could only see his face.

"How are you so good-looking?" I asked for the millionth time.

"I have to be." He pushed his own goggles back and met my eyes. "Have you seen yourself?"

I chewed on my bottom lip. "You mean it?"

"I've always meant it." As he scooted closer, snow crunched in a soft rhythm. He bit a finger of his glove and pulled his hand out. His warm fingers caressed my cool cheek, making the touch that much more powerful.

I kept eye contact with him, wanting to know if our connection affected him as much as it did me.

Because I could live and die in this single moment where Jon looked at me like the sun rose and set in my eyes.

"I hope you know this is it for me," Jon said. "*You're* it for me."

But I didn't have time to respond because there was a black figure flying around the bend in the trail, too fast. Out of control. And he was heading right for us.

Skis and poles flew through the air, and a body crashed into us, screaming on the way. Jon let out a guttural cry that would forever be seared in my mind. And the cry didn't end. Even after the person rolled to a stop in a crumpled heap, moaning.

Blood seeped into the snow. Covered Jon's ungloved hand that was now gripping his leg, the spot where something that should not have been there protruded from his snow pants.

"HELP!" I screamed, knowing if I reached for my phone, which didn't have service on the mountaintop, it wouldn't do me any good. I didn't quit screaming until an EMT was there with us. Strapping Jon to a board. Telling me to wait for another snowmobile. Leaving me alone on the trail by a patch of blood-soaked snow, wondering how, or if, Jon would ever be okay.

CHAPTER TWENTY

I WAS DESPERATELY TAPPING at my phone, wishing for there to be service, when someone on a snowmobile arrived. I fumbled with my board, but it slid away from me. Crashed into a tree before falling down the mountainside.

"Leave it," the man said.

He didn't need to tell me twice.

I flung my body over the back of the snowmobile, suddenly ready to do whatever was needed to get to Jon. The snowmobile took us down the slopes faster than I ever could have managed on my board.

When we neared the bottom, my phone went off. Over and over again with voicemail messages. I didn't dare retrieve it from my pocket and open them now for fear of losing my phone.

He dropped me off at the lodge, and I immediately dialed Grandma's number. Everyone around me seemed to be going on like everything was completely normal and fine. I hated them for that.

Her voice was frantic. "Abi, what happened?"

"Someone crashed into us!" I cried. "Where is he?"

"They're flying him to Santa Fe," Grandma said. "He's lost a lot of blood already."

"Where are you?" I asked.

"In Jon's car at the lodge. Right out front."

I ran as fast as I could in those stupid boots, but the stairs fought me. I crashed down, banging my knee and shoulder on the way. But there wasn't time for pain or clumsiness. I forced myself up and hurried to the car. Jorge was standing at the driver's side, gripping the door.

He yelled, "Are you—"

"I'm fine," I shouted. "Let's *go!*"

I slid into the back seat. Why wasn't he driving faster already? I needed to see Jon. Needed to know he was okay. That his face contorted in pain and his strangled cry wouldn't be the last thing I ever saw or heard from him.

"Hurry!" I said.

Jorge put the car in drive and took off.

"What happened?" Grandma asked, twisting in her seat.

I shook my head, trying to get a grasp on my breath. "We were just lying there, taking a break, and this skier came around the corner—crashed into us. He hit Jon first..." I closed my eyes against the blood on the ground and Jon's cries. "Have they said anything about Jon? Will he be okay?"

Grandma reached around and gripped my knee. "All we know is that he has a ski pole lodged in his thigh. They're taking him to the hospital in Santa Fe."

I pressed the heels of my hands into my closed eyes. This was all my fault, thinking I needed to "live." Whatever the hell that meant. Who said just being with Jon wasn't living? It would be better than this. Every second not knowing how he was felt like dying. I would never trade slapping some plywood to my legs and sliding down some snow for this. Never.

Jorge started down the winding mountain roads, and all I could think was that this was too slow. I needed to be with Jon. Needed to hear the doctor say he would be okay. Instead, we rode in complete silence for more than two hours, without receiving a single call from Marta or Glen.

We finally arrived at the hospital, and as we stepped out of the car, Grandma commanded, "Go."

She and Jorge wouldn't be able to keep up with me where Jon was concerned. With her one-word blessing, I sprinted through the emergency entrance and skidded to a stop at the reception desk. "Jon Scoller. Which room is he in?"

She looked at her computer screen, no hint of urgency in her motions. "He's in OR. You can wait in the ICU lobby."

"Where?"

A door swung open to my right, and she half stood to point. "Around the corner, to the right. Follow the green line."

My head spun as I attempted to walk straight. Operating room? Jon was in surgery?

I turned the final corner and reached the end of the green line. With their heads bowed in prayer and hands latched together, were Glen and Marta. A sob escaped my throat.

Marta caught sight of me and sprang to action. She came to me, wrapped an arm around my shoulder, and walked me to sit beside them. I was still wearing those stupid snowboard boots.

I began yanking at them, desperate to get them off.

"Abi, Abi, Abi," Marta said, her hands covering mine.

I collapsed over my knees, sobbing. "I'm so sorry."

She took my chin and lifted my gaze to hers. "It wasn't your fault."

She'd never said he'd be okay.

She'd never said he'd recover.

Or that he'd run again.

All she'd said was that it wasn't my fault. Whatever *it* meant, I wouldn't find out until Jon came out of surgery.

CHAPTER TWENTY-ONE

FOR THE LONGEST four hours of my life, we waited in the lobby, all huddled together, refusing food, drinking stale hospital coffee, dreading bad news and praying for good.

There were a couple other families who got word of their loved ones before us. I couldn't help but listen to the prognoses given, watch the way they reacted. I desperately wanted to be one of the families who received a positive outcome. And when a doctor came out and said, "Scoller," I dreaded what we were about to find out.

"Are you family?" he asked the group.

"Yes," Marta answered.

He looked skeptical, but tucked his clipboard under his side. "Jonathan suffered severe trauma to his right thigh that barely missed his bone. We had to remove the pole and do our best to reconstruct several muscles and ligaments. We want to keep him in the trauma unit until we can move him to recovery."

"Do you know how long it will be?" Marta asked.

I was glad her mind was working, because mine was still stuck on "severe trauma." On his leg muscles that had needed reconstruction. And on the fact that running was everything to Jon. Everything.

"We expect he'll be here for a week, and then we'll get him set up with a physical therapist local to you."

She nodded.

"His attending physician will help sort that out."

She nodded again.

"Will he be able to run after this?" I asked.

The surgeon cringed. "He's a collegiate track athlete, am I correct?"

I nodded.

"He might be able to run for fun someday, but competitively? The odds aren't great. His PT will be able to explain that more."

My heart crashed to the speckled hospital floor and shattered. "Does Jon know?"

"He hasn't been awake for us to tell him. Would you prefer to do that?"

"Yes," Glen spoke up and gripped Marta's shoulder. "When can we go see him?"

"He'll be waking up soon, and then they'll move him to his new room." He scanned his clipboard. "4021. Feel free to wait up there or run some errands if you need to."

It seemed cruel to use the word "run" in a moment like this.

He asked if we had any more questions, and when we didn't, he turned tail and left. I wanted to be angry at him, but all I could manage was anger with myself. Jon wouldn't have even been there if it weren't for me.

As if she could hear my thoughts, Grandma laced her fingers through mine and squeezed. "Let's go upstairs?"

I nodded, sending tears falling down my cheeks.

We all walked to the elevators together and pushed the button for the trauma floor. The doors opened to the louder chaos of this floor, which stood out against the quiet hustle of the ICU. There were families visiting in rooms, a patient screaming for help down the hall, and then there was Jon's room,

4021. While no sound came from within, it might as well have been crying out at me.

Marta paused outside the door and looked back at us. "Would you mind giving us a moment with our son?"

"Of course," Grandma replied, at the same moment I froze.

I wanted to be in there with him. But he wasn't just mine. At least, not yet. He was theirs too. He was still their son. I was just the girlfriend, sliding a not-engagement ring around my finger.

Grandma squeezed my hand tighter and pulled me away, toward the lobby. I couldn't stand lobbies anymore, but it looked like I didn't have a choice.

Jorge looked between the two of us. "Can I get you anything? Coffee? Food?"

"No," I said at the same time Grandma said, "Yes."

"Yes," Grandma said again. "Please get us something light to eat."

"Grandma, I said no."

"Look at me," she ordered, her eyes intense. "That boy in there is the love of your life, right?"

"Right," I said without hesitation.

"This is what a lasting relationship is," she said. "It's more than vacations and birthday presents. It's being there for each other during the hard times. Taking care of yourself so you *can* be there during the hard times."

I swallowed, nodded. "I'll take a sandwich. And some water."

"Good." Grandma hugged me to her side.

Jorge nodded at her, pure admiration in his features. He wasn't Grandpa, but he was good for her. Somehow, he leveled out her bossy personality while marveling at her strength. I liked that. There needed to be a bright spot in this horrible situation.

After I shoved a sandwich that might as well have been cardboard down my throat and drank a whole bottle of water, we sat, and we waited.

And finally, Marta and Glen came to the lobby.

Marta looked to me and said, "Jon wants to see you."

CHAPTER TWENTY-TWO

MY LEGS SHOOK as I walked down the hallway to 4021. My entire life was in that room, and he had just found out that his had been ruined.

There would be no way to comfort him. No way to face him with a cheery outlook. I had to be comfortable sitting in his pain, but I didn't know how to do that. I wanted to take it away. Why couldn't I have been lying on that side for the skier to crash into? I wanted to go to college, sure, but not as badly as Jon. I wasn't as good at track as him. Wasn't as passionate as him. I'd take all his pain and more a million times over if it meant he didn't have to.

I finally reached the door and took a deep, steadying breath before walking in.

Jon almost looked normal, if it weren't for the

bulging underneath the blanket. Whether it was a brace or a cast, I didn't know, but I knew it shouldn't have been there.

His eyes met mine, looking lost, defeated, and I covered my mouth, tears choking out any of my words. Not that there were any words for this moment. None that would be good enough.

"Abi," he said, and it decimated the dam.

I went to him, kneeling next to the bed and taking both of his hands in mine.

"You know?" he said.

I nodded.

And he broke.

We broke, sobbing together over everything he'd hoped for and everything he'd lost in a fraction of a second.

How long we cried, I didn't know, but when we finally stopped, I made him a promise. "We'll figure this out. Together."

His voice was small. "If I never run again...if I never race. Would you still want me?"

There was only one answer. "Yes. Running might be everything to you, but you are everything to me."

He held my hands to his cheek, and my heart

shattered even more completely at the moisture there.

"You have no idea how much that means," he said, his voice rough.

I stayed silent, because there was nothing else to say. I had to make good of my promise to be here.

Eventually, Jon's breathing slowed, and soft snores escaped his lips. From exhaustion or the medication he was undoubtedly on, I didn't know. Still, I held on to his hand. Despite him losing something so enormous, gratitude overwhelmed me. Jon was here. He was okay. I could never be thankful enough for that truth.

Footsteps fell in the hallway, and Grandma was there. She came to stand beside me at Jon's bed, rubbing my shoulder.

"How's he taking it?" she whispered.

I just shook my head, on the verge of tears yet again.

"Marta said he shut down. Asked for you."

Some strange, selfish part of me was pleased at that news.

"We're going to go get our things from the lodge and find a hotel closer to the hospital," Grandma said. "Marta and Glen are coming with us. Are you good here?"

I looked back at Jon and his serene face. At least in his sleep he could escape. "We'll be fine. I can call if anything new happens."

She nodded, squeezed my shoulder. "I'm proud of you, Abi." She kissed the top of my head.

My lips trembled. "Thank you."

And then I settled into the nearest chair and watched Jon sleep, wishing the peaceful look on his face could stay with him during what I knew would be incredibly hard weeks and months to come.

* * *

At some point, I fell asleep. I woke up to Jon shifting in the bed, moaning.

My eyes snapped open. "What's happening?"

"It hurts," he groaned.

Scrambling, I searched for the call button and finally found it hanging over the bedrails. After a moment, a voice came over the line. "Yes?"

"We need pain medicine. Now."

"We'll be there soon."

"Thank you," I said and then gripped Jon's fingers even tighter. "Squeeze my hand if you need to."

He did. Hard. But I welcomed the pain. I

wanted him holding on to something if he couldn't hold on to hope.

"Soon" in the hospital didn't mean "soon" to an outsider. Five minutes passed. Ten, then thirty. I called the nurse again, and they said it was shift change. My voice shook with anger as I told them my boyfriend was in pain.

"We'll be there soon," they said.

"I don't want soon, I want—"

The line went dead.

Jon had gone from shifting and moaning to gritting his teeth and lying stiff as a board. Every muscle in his arms was taut.

Finally, a nurse walked in, taking her sweet time to give him medicine that would surely take time to kick in. Grandma was right; I needed my strength to deal with this, to advocate for him. It made me wonder what it had been like for her in the final months of Grandpa's life, while he'd suffered in a hospital bed.

CHAPTER TWENTY-THREE

FOR THE NEXT WEEK, days blended into nights, and the date or time became irrelevant. It was about waking and sleeping and managing pain and checking with the surgeon to make sure healing was taking place and swelling was going down. Texting our friends to give them updates, none substantially new or different.

And then they released him early in the morning, the day before New Year's Eve.

Jon and I rode in the car with his parents while Grandma and Jorge drove his car home. Thankfully, Jon slept most of the way, his leg propped up on the center console.

I sat beside him, trying to get lost in music and

books, but mostly getting caught in the unsure web of our future. Of my fears.

When we got back to Woodman, Marta sent me home for a nap and a shower. Grandma went to help in my place, even though Marta more than had it covered.

I showered, as they asked, and then crawled in my bed, wishing for this nightmare to be over. To wake up from it.

No such luck.

I walked to Jon's house the next evening after having slept for more than twelve hours. Even after a good meal and two cups of coffee, I still felt groggy. At least the cold air helped with that.

Outside the Scollers' house, it looked prepped for their traditional New Year's Eve party that doubled as Jon's birthday bash. Lights hung along the guttering, and each of the frogs on their lawn donned party hats atop their metal heads. I pictured Jon inside, wearing a sweater that clung to his shoulders, but my fantasy broke where I'd normally be drooling over his jeans. This time, there would be shorts there, compression socks, an immobilization brace, and crutches.

I prepared myself for that. But when I opened

the door, I saw the one negative scenario I hadn't prepared myself for.

Denise.

CHAPTER TWENTY-FOUR

I STARED at her where she conversed with Marta and Glen, standing with Leanne and Macy, like she belonged in this house, anywhere near Jon.

Marta noticed me and stepped away from them to greet me. "You're looking so much better, honey." She gave my arm an encouraging rub.

I returned the gesture with a weak smile. It had been hard to miss the dark circles growing under my eyes in the last week. I felt at least ten years older. "How's he doing?"

The lines around her eyes creased. "As well as can be expected." She reached out and took his present from me. "I'll set this on the table. Allow yourself to enjoy the party tonight, okay?"

I nodded, even though I had a surprise visitor

and Jon's condition joining forces against me. I had
meant to bypass Denise on the way to the kitchen,
but she had her steely eyes narrowed in on me.

"Abi," she said, blocking the doorway. "How are
you? How's college?"

Leanne and Macy watched me, waiting to see
what I would do with the false kindness she'd
displayed.

I could play this game. Maybe not as well as if I
hadn't just sat by Jon's hospital bed for an entire
week, watching him suffer, but still. "I'm doing
great!" I forced out with a smile. "Considering the
circumstances. You heard about my boyfriend?"

Her smooth expression broke at the term. I
counted it a win. But she quickly recovered and said,
"I heard Jon got hurt trying to teach you to ski.
Weren't y'all being careful? I know it's so hard to
learn when you're not naturally coordinated."

Okay, point Denise. But what was she playing
at? More importantly, who was she playing for?

I lowered my voice, deciding to swing just as low
as she had. "We just snuck off for a little...time
together, and this skier was out of control. Thanks for
your concern. We've got him all taken care of."

And then I walked away. If Denise wanted to go
another round, she'd have to chase me for the chance.

Stormy quickly appeared at my side. "Gah, I can't stand Denise. How she and Leanne share DNA, I have no idea."

"I mean, it's not like Leanne's all sunshine and rainbows." I stopped at the cider dispenser and poured myself a glass, purely for something to do with my hands.

Stormy leaned back against the island. "True. But at least Leanne's not evil."

"And she's not trying to steal Jon back."

"It would be kind of pointless, considering he has a penis and all."

I laughed. Finally. It felt foreign. "Speaking of penises, have you seen Jon yet?"

She shook her head. "Frank's upstairs with him in his room. I think they're watching a movie."

I nodded, sad that Jon had isolated himself that way. He was usually the life of the party, making everyone feel at home in the media room.

"They're fine up there. But what about you?" she said, rubbing my arm. "How are you doing? This can't be easy."

Moisture sprang to my eyes. It always seemed to be at the ready these days. "I'm worried about him."

She pulled me into a hug, her growing stomach

pressing against my waist. "You're the strongest person I know. He's lucky to have you."

"Lucky isn't the word I'd use to describe him."

Her mouth twisted to the side. "Maybe not right now. But he is."

I hoped she was right, but I couldn't see how. I needed to change the subject, or I'd fall apart right here and be an even bigger puddle than the punch bowl. "Where are the others?"

She knew who I meant. Our friends. My rocks. She counted off on her fingers. "Freckles, Andrew, and Skye are on the back porch, drinking cider with rum. Those jerks. Macy and Leanne agreed to babysit the *enemy*, Roberto's already back in NC, and you know where Frank is."

"And Michele?" I asked.

"Coming soon, I think."

I nodded. "Let's go outside?"

"You don't want to see Jon?"

I did, but... "I think it would be good for him to have some guy time."

She put her arm around me. "And you need some friend time."

We walked together outside and sat on the back porch with Andrew, Skye, and Evan.

Evan nudged my arm. "You good?" he asked low.

I shrugged.

"Come on," he said, draining his cup and standing up. "I have something for you in my car."

"Sure."

We told our friends we'd be back and walked to his SUV. I was going to wait on the sidewalk for him to get whatever it was, but he opened the door for me so I could get in.

I did, and when he sat in the driver's side, turning on the vehicle, I looked over at him, confused. "What are we doing out here?"

Concern was plain in his dark brown eyes, even in the low light cast from the streetlights. "You looked like you could use a second away from it all."

The tears that were always there came back, and I stared at him. How did he know?

I sobbed into my hands, all of it finally hitting me. That life would be forever different for Jon, for me—for us.

Evan turned off the car and got out, stunning me out of my tears. Where was he going?

Soon, he was on my side, opening the door. "Come to the back seat," he said. "I can't hug you here."

I half laughed, half sobbed and did as he asked. We sat in the back seat, him cradling me and holding me tight and letting me be the weak one for the first time in seven days. I cried into his chest, and he stroked my hair, never asking for explanations or offering empty fixes.

By the time my sobs finally slowed, the windows were fogged, and my eyes burned. I looked up at Evan and thanked him. I couldn't be grateful enough for this burden he'd lifted off of me, if only for a little while.

"Any time," he said and kissed the top of my head.

The car door jerked open, and there stood Michele, mouth open in horror. "I knew it."

The bigger problem? Denise was right behind her.

CHAPTER TWENTY-FIVE

AS DENISE SPRINTED BACK toward the house, I sat frozen, torn between backing up Evan and stopping whatever lies Denise would spread once she got inside. Of course, that meant I sat there, mouth gaping, making Evan and me look guiltier than we were.

"How could you?" Michele demanded.

I had to believe Jon would trust me enough to know the truth. And Evan had been a real friend.

"Michele," I said, "we were just talking in the car." The tears on my face made my skin sting from the cold. I wiped at them and looked toward the sky. "He was helping me with this mess. It's just a misunderstanding."

She ignored me, staring at Evan instead. "Was

this your plan all along? Bide your time until she was heartbroken and then be her knight in shining armor?"

"What?" Evan's face screwed up with incredulity. "No, M, that's not even close to true."

"Really," I said. "I'm with Jon, I love Jon, I would never try to risk that."

Michele rolled her eyes. "Yeah, that's why you're always flirting with Evan and Roberto right in front of him."

My head jerked back with the force of her accusation. "Flirting? What are you talking about?"

"Like you don't know," she scoffed. "There's a reason you're out here with Evan instead of in there with Jon."

"Yeah, because Evan's my friend, and Jon's a big boy. He can handle a few minutes away from me."

"Sure," she countered. "Like he hasn't just been waiting to get Denise back after he saw what you didn't have to offer beneath the sheets."

I couldn't even breathe through all the red in front of me. Michele had no idea what I'd been through, what I'd overcome, what Jon and I shared. And now she had the nerve to act like Denise could swoop in one night at a party and shatter it all?

Whoever did her lobotomy needed to be slapped. Right after her.

I stepped forward, hand raised, ready to put her in her place—preferably on the ground.

"Enough!" Evan yelled. "Michele, it's over. I'm tired of you constantly being jealous of Abi. She's my friend, but if you don't trust me, there's nothing here." He waved his hand between the two of them. "I can't be with someone who doesn't take me at my word or let me spend time with my friends." He looked at me. "And I expected more from you than to stoop to her level."

He pushed past the two of us and got in his car. The tires squealed as he peeled off, leaving Michele and me standing in the street. She looked stunned, like a deer in the headlights with her doe eyes wide and mouth slightly open.

Even though she'd said some horrible things, I felt bad for her. She clearly liked Evan. And he was right. How could I have been ready to do the same thing my parents did to me? "Michele, I—"

"No." She held up her hand. "There's nothing you can do to make me feel better. But don't worry, you'll know exactly how I feel by the end of the night."

With that, she ran toward her car and got in.

Now I was alone, the sounds of the party finally registering in my ears. I looked up at the window I knew was Jon's, at the figures moving behind the curtains. Jon would believe me.

He had to.

Right?

CHAPTER TWENTY-SIX

I WALKED up the stairs to Jon's room, my head pounding with fear. I didn't know what Denise had done, but I knew she was the master manipulator. If she wanted Jon back—or to get even for him leaving her for me—she would pull out all the stops. She would give everything in her effort and more.

And Jon was vulnerable right now, hurting. The perfect timing, like Michele had suggested for Evan and me.

I slowed in the hallway and crept toward his room, hoping I'd be able to hear some of the conversation inside. Maybe if I knew what she said, I'd know how to make him see the truth.

There were two voices, one low, Jon's, and one feminine. Denise.

Someone whispered behind me, "What are you doing, Abi?"

I sprang forward, nearly falling on my face in Jon's open doorway. "God, Frank, you scared me."

He chuckled silently like my near heart attack was the funniest thing in the world.

I punched his arm because it wasn't. "You're stupid."

He lifted the two bottles of water in his hands and shrugged. "Yeah, but I'm funny."

"That's up for debate."

The voices in Jon's room had quieted now. They must have heard us.

Frank gestured toward the door, and I went first. Denise sat on Jon's bed, her hand on his immobilization brace. The sight of it was enough to make me want to vomit. God forbid she stand on the other side of the room or disappear like I wanted her to.

When she saw me, she didn't make any motions to back away from Jon. I looked away from her to Jon, who had a concerned expression clouding his eyes.

"I need to talk with Abi," he announced. "Now."

The strength in his voice made Denise jump. "But Jon—"

"No," he said. "Get out."

The harshness in his words surprised me too. Jon almost never sounded that angry. What had she told him?

Frank handed Jon a water bottle and said, "Crush you at GTA later?"

Jon nodded, but left it at that, his green eyes on me.

The second the door closed, I said, "What did Denise tell you?"

He pushed himself further up on the bed and folded his arms. "What do you think she told me?"

I rubbed my face, exhausted. "I'd rather not play games. But probably something horrible that's going to make you want to leave me more than you already do."

My voice shook on those last words, and I had to look down. Jon hadn't said he wanted to leave, never suggested he thought the injury was my fault, but I felt guilty nonetheless. If he didn't feel like leaving me, like I'd ruined his life, he should.

He was silent for too long, so long I had to look up at him. I watched his emotions go from frustrated to conflicted to full of feeling.

He spread his arms wide. "Come here."

I looked at him, tears springing to my eyes yet again. "What?"

"Come here," he repeated.

So I did as he asked and carefully climbed into bed next to him. He lifted the blanket over the two of us and wrapped me in his arms. For a moment, we stayed that way, breathing in the muted hum of the party below and the warmth passing between us.

But I still felt unsettled. "Don't you want to know what happened out there?" I finally asked.

He shook his head, his chin rubbing against the top of my head. "Not particularly."

"What?" I craned my neck to look at him.

He looked down, meeting me eyes. "Should I be worried?"

"Well...no, but Denise—"

"I don't care about Denise," he said, anger tinting his voice and then simmering. "I care about us, here and now. Abi, I'm never going to run again. Do you really think I'm going to risk losing everything I have left over something a jealous ex-girlfriend tells me?"

A light laugh escaped my lips at the absurdity of it. Jon was right. He knew Denise just as well as I did —better. And he was finally seeing through her act. Maybe things between us would go back to normal soon. He would see he had a life outside of running. At least, I hoped.

CHAPTER TWENTY-SEVEN

JON SAT ON MY BED, his leg elevated on a pile of pillows, while I packed my bags full of freshly done laundry. We had to leave for college the day after next for track practice, since athletes didn't get as long of a break as other students.

My phone chimed with a text message. I set a stack of winter sweaters in my suitcase and then went to my dresser to see who it was.

Stormy: I want to see you before you go back. Come over?

Abi: I'll see if Jon's up for it.

Stormy: Let's just do girl time, okay? I'd ask Frank to hang out with Jon, but he's working.

Abi: Sure. I can come over after I finish packing.

"Who is it?" Jon asked.

I set my phone back on the dresser. "Stormy. She wants some girl time before I go back."

He frowned. "Girl time?"

"Yeah." I shrugged. "Maybe she wants to talk about baby stuff. Or Frank."

"Sounds stimulating."

I threw a winter hat at him.

"Seriously," he said, tossing it back. "Why didn't you ask me first?"

I paused over my suitcase. Saying *you're not my dad* seemed a little much in this situation, but I was tempted. "What do you mean?" I asked instead.

"I mean, we were going to hang out today, and you just decided to drop me. You don't have a hot date with Freckles, do you?"

The hurt on his face was clear, even through the poorly made joke. "It's not that at all." I went to him, holding his hand. "I'll show you the texts if you want."

He didn't say no. So I got my phone from the dresser, opening up the texting screen.

He glanced over the messages, barely masking a look of relief when he saw it was actually Stormy.

"See?" I said, taking it back. "It's not about you."

"I knew that much already." Cringing, he moved

his leg from the pillow tower and sat up. "I'm going back home."

"I'm not leaving yet," I said, an ache forming in my heart.

"I know." He forced a smile. I could tell because it didn't reach his eyes like usual. "I'll see you later."

"When?" I asked.

"As soon as you want to see me. If you do."

He hobbled out of the room on crutches, and I couldn't help the stinging lump that formed in my throat. I tried to swallow it down, along with an added dose of guilt, and went back to packing.

The front door closed, and a knock sounded on my doorframe. I looked up to see Grandma there, her head leaning against the wood trim and a basket of laundry resting on her hip. "How ya holding up, hon?"

I shook my head, sending a tear dripping down my nose. I groaned, more frustrated with myself than anything. Jon was right. We were spending time together. Why hadn't I asked him what he thought?

Grandma walked in and set the laundry basket on my bed. "It's been a tough time for everyone."

"You can say that again." I sniffed.

"You know what they say. When it rains, it pours."

"Well, it feels like monsoon season," I muttered and sat on my bed to sort through the laundry.

"You've always been good at finding an umbrella," she said pointedly. "And I just want you to know that I'm proud of you."

My lips trembled, and my hand stilled on a T-shirt. I didn't feel very proud of myself right now. I'd ruined Jon's track career, ruined Evan's relationship...What would I ruin next? I looked up at her, searching for the truth behind her words. She'd meant every one.

* * *

I walked into Stormy's house and found her in her room, a bowl of popcorn on her swollen stomach.

"Should you be eating sodium?" I asked.

She glared at me.

I put my hands up like a shield—I had a feeling I might need one soon—and said, "I meant to say, do you need a foot rub?"

"That's more like it." She laughed and patted the bed beside her.

I obliged and got on the mattress. For a second, I listened to her pop the snack in her mouth and crunch it.

"Jon didn't want me to come here," I blurted.

She looked over at me, a piece of popcorn caught on her top lip. "What do you mean?"

"He thought I should have asked first." I reached over and flicked it off.

She rolled her eyes. "I didn't know he was a caveman."

"I didn't either." I grabbed some popcorn myself and popped it in my mouth, savoring the flood of flavor while I chewed over my feelings. "Do you think it's just because he's hurting?"

She thought it over for a second. "I mean, maybe?"

"Ugh." I lay back on her bed and stared at the ceiling. "This is awful."

"That's it." She had a turtle moment as she tried to sit up but didn't get the momentum.

She had no idea how good of a friend I was for not laughing.

"What?" I asked.

"We're getting out of here," she said. "Frank's not here to baby me, and you're not wallowing inside. Let's go out."

"And do what?" I asked. "It's Woodman, and we're nineteen."

"I don't know." She flung her arms out. "A movie, dinner? Shopping for some slutty outfits?"

I rolled my eyes at the last comment. "But I could use a few clothes that aren't sweatpants."

"That too," she said. "When we get out of the house, you'll feel better."

And she was right. After an hour walking around the strip mall, my anxiety had eased, if only slightly. Retail therapy had to be a real thing. And at least I wouldn't leave a "session" feeling completely wiped.

That was, until we ran into two of the people at the bottom of my list.

I ducked behind a stand of clothes and waved Stormy to follow me, but she defiantly craned her head around. "Who's here?"

Farther down the aisle, Denise and Michele consulted each other, and Michele grabbed Denise's hand, walking determinedly toward us. I didn't know when they'd become friends, but I really hated it.

I realized I must have looked stupid hiding behind a frame and stood straighter, muttering, "Five o'clock."

"Great," Stormy grumbled.

They strutted up, their chests puffed out like it somehow made them more menacing.

Stormy cut them off before they could speak. "What do Paris and Nicole want today?"

"Who?" Michele asked.

Denise pointed at me. "We want to talk to *her*."

"Oh please," Stormy groaned. "Take your high school drama elsewhere. We have real problems to worry about." She grabbed my hand and turned away.

Denise cocked an eyebrow. "Like your bastard child?"

Stormy froze, fire behind her eyes. She could have kicked Denise's ass, pregnant or not.

Even though part of me wanted her to, I held her arm so she had to stay put. I turned to face them. "Get it over with, Denise. What do you two want?"

They looked between each other like they weren't expecting me to agree.

"Well," Michele began, lifting her chest again, "I want an explanation."

"Of what?" I said. "The fact that Evan was my friend before he was your boyfriend? And, while I think of it, the same goes for you and Jon, Denise."

They both stared at me, stunned. I took advantage and kept going. "Michele, I know literally nothing about you. Mostly because I don't care. If Evan likes you, I'm fine with it. But there's a reason he didn't chase you last night. And there's a reason you're talking to me now instead of him."

She folded her arms across her chest, clenching her jaw and staring hard at a mannequin.

"If you care about him, you'll back off me and work things out with *him*. I'm with Jon. I love Jon. I'm going to marry *Jon*."

Everyone's jaws dropped.

"What?" I asked. I knew I wasn't that profound.

Stormy elbowed me. "Is there something you're not telling me?"

"Huh?"

"Married?" Denise squeaked.

Oh. That was it. "I mean, someday, yeah." My cheeks reddened. If this got back to Jon...

Denise stepped forward. "It doesn't change the fact that you stole Jon from me. What, was Evan not good enough for you? Was he too available?"

Stormy let out the most exasperated sigh I'd ever heard, but I shook my head. This wasn't about Michele or Evan at all. It was between Denise and me. I stared at her now, at the eyeliner too thick along her lashes and the jutted jaw that she used to hide how insecure she really was.

I tried to make her understand. "Look, Denise. You know I used to be so jealous of you—of how Jon felt about you, but I couldn't do anything about how skinny you were or that you always wore cute clothes and big sunglasses. I could only work on me. I don't know why, but he picked me. He *chose* me."

Denise's eyes were bright red now as she looked me over. "But, why you?"

Shaking my head, I shrugged. "I'll let you know when I figure it out."

Denise and Michele looked between each other, and Michele muttered, "Let's go."

With a final examination of me and a trembling lip, Denise turned and followed her friend.

My shoulders sagged. I'd won. I'd managed a confrontation, stood up for myself, but I didn't feel happy. I was sorry for them. I knew how it hurt to love a guy and not feel good enough—to look for problems. But I had other things to worry about right now.

Popcorn crunched beside me as Stormy shoved a fistful in her mouth.

I stared at her, slack jawed. "Where did that even come from?"

Swallowing her popcorn, she said, "What? Catfights make me hungry."

It was the funniest thing I'd heard all day.

Stormy let out a scream, dropping hangers of

clothes on the floor. "THE BABY MOVED! SHE MOVED!" She folded over her stomach, like she could hold the baby in her arms.

"What?" I cried. "No way!"

She smiled over at me, an evil glint in her shining eyes. "She's going to be a handful. Already likes drama."

CHAPTER TWENTY-EIGHT

I WANTED to tell Jon about my encounter with his ex, but when I texted him, he just sent me clipped answers. I tried heading over to his house that evening, but Marta said he was already asleep.

I gave up, resigned to the fact that I'd have to wait until our drive back to Austin the next day. Knowing we'd have two hours in a car together to sort it out didn't make sleeping any easier, so when the Scollers picked Gram and me up for breakfast the next morning, I was less than chipper.

I downed at least three cups of coffee along with my eggs and wholegrain toast, and even took one for the road, which I finished by the time we got back to their house. Marta gave me more than a few concerned looks.

As we pulled into their driveway, Glen looked at me in the rear-view mirror. "We want to speak with you and Jon," he said, then opened the door and got out.

I couldn't see Jon's expression from where I sat in the back, but I wondered if he was as confused as I was. I tried to gauge Gram's reaction, but she was already walking toward the house. Apparently, she was in on this.

Jon and I followed up the group, walking slowly because he was on crutches.

In a hushed voice, I asked, "Do you know what this is about?"

"Not a clue," he muttered.

Had they found out we were having sex? We hadn't since Jon's injury, but still. Maybe Marta was serious about us waiting until marriage. Or they finally wanted to chastise me for putting Jon in a position to be injured. They hadn't yelled at me yet, so it was high time. I wouldn't even blame them.

When we reached the living room, Marta said we should sit on the loveseat across from the sofa. All that was missing was an interrogation lamp and two-way mirrors.

Jon put his crutches together and lowered himself down. "What's this about, Mom?"

Glen folded his hands in his lap. "This was my idea."

"But it has my full support," Marta said, and Grandma nodded.

My brows came together. What was going on here?

Glen took a breath. "I think it might be wise for you both to take the semester off. You've been through a lot. Jon, you just came out of the hospital. Abi, there's the trial coming up. And your father's parole hearing. You're going to have to miss classes, practices. There are going to be people asking you questions you don't have answers for. They're going to try to get you to admit to things you didn't do. They'll accuse you of being a charlatan, drawing that boy out to the country and provoking him. Of provoking your father. It will be messy."

I gaped at him. "Provoking my dad to beat me?"

He gritted his teeth, but didn't deny it. "Honey, I think you have bigger things to worry about than school and track this semester. Marta and I will worry about your tuition if you can't get back on the team next year."

My mouth opened and closed like a drawbridge blocking confounded words from spilling over my tongue. I turned to Jon. What did he think about this?

His jaw worked, the muscle there twitching. "You can't be serious."

"I am, son," Glen said. "Abi was incredibly brave to finish the semester after what happened, but it's only going to get harder."

Harder than running for my life on the Mexico border? He had to be kidding.

Jon stood up, grabbing his crutches. "No. Abi's given up so much already, and you want her to what? Give up track, lose all the momentum she's worked to gain?"

Mr. Scoller worked his jaw. "You might think running in a circle is all life has to offer—"

"What about you?" Jon demanded of Grandma. "I can't believe you'd support this."

Her voice was firm as she glared between Jon and Glen. "I support what *Abi* decides is best for her." Then she looked directly at me. "Whatever you decide, sweetheart, I'm here for you."

The tension in my chest eased, knowing she meant what she said because Jon was right. I'd been through hell and back to get where I was now. Staying home would just be admitting defeat. I needed to go, to prove to myself that I could do this. That I really did have my freedom.

"I want to go back to college," I said.

"The trial—" Glen began, but I shook my head.

"I have a good therapist in place; I'm doing well in track. I don't want to let all that go," I said. "And no one's told us when the trial starts, much less when the parole hearing is. They could both be this summer for all we know."

The three adults exchanged a look.

Acid rose in my throat. "What?" I demanded.

Grandma worried her hands in her lap. "Eric's first hearing is in two months. You've been subpoenaed as a witness."

Jon dropped onto the couch beside me. "Wow."

Too many thoughts came at me at once, and a buzzing sound crowded out any hopes of sorting them out. The trial. Dad. Jon. Evan and Michele. It was like they were all torpedoing my brain, trying to gain access but failing because there was just too much.

Jon's voice cut the noise. "Abi?" He took my hand in his and lowered his voice, just talking to me. "What do you want? I'll do whatever you want." The desperation I heard behind his words almost scared me.

All of my thoughts snapped into action, slammed into place. "I want to go." I stood and gave Grandma and the Scollers quick, awkward hugs. "I'll see you soon."

I took the keys to Jon's car off the hook by the door, marched down the sidewalk, and sat in the driver's seat, waiting for him to come outside. My bags could stay here. I could live with what I left in the dorms.

When Jon came out, he was smart enough to stay silent, to let me process.

For the first part of the drive, Jon held my hand, knowing I needed his presence more than his words. But eventually, I needed to talk, and not just about the trial.

"What is going on with you?" I asked.

Jon looked down at his leg. "That's what you want to talk about? With everything we just heard inside?"

I pressed on anyway. "You've never been upset about me hanging out with my friends before or thought I should ask permission. And you've *never* wanted to see my messages."

My unspoken question hung between us, palpable. *Was this our new normal?*

"I don't know." His head hung as he stared at his

hands. "I think I've just been leaning on you a lot lately. Ever since…what happened, we've hardly been apart. It surprised me you could leave so easily."

Suddenly, Jon looked smaller than usual. More like someone I needed to protect than someone I typically relied on for strength.

How could I support him the way he needed— and deserved—when a constant state of panic welled below the surface of my consciousness?

But I had to figure it out, because this was part of a relationship.

Right? Give and take? Giving all you had when the other person had nothing left?

"Jon." I looked at him as long as I could while driving. "I don't know how I can help or what you need, but I'm here for you. Whatever you need, I'm here."

He stared out the window and wiped at his eyes before turning back to me, his voice raw as he spoke. "I just need you."

CHAPTER TWENTY-NINE

THE CIRCLES under Jon's eyes told me he'd slept just as poorly as I had. We walked quietly together to track practice, leaving twenty minutes early to give him a chance to speak with his coach.

He tried to keep an even expression, but I could tell this was killing him inside. I couldn't even hold his hand because of the crutches, so I settled for matching his pace, willing him to understand how much I loved him.

When we reached the hallway with his coach's office, I said, "Wait."

Jon settled on his crutches, looking at me.

"I need to say this, and I think you need to hear it." I reached up and put a hand on his smooth cheek. "You are more than your ability to run."

His eyes filled before he quickly blinked away the tears.

"I'm here for you whatever happens in that room," I said, glancing down the hall. "I promise."

He adjusted his crutches so he could cover my hand with his own. "That means more than you know."

I gave him a half-hearted smile, and he turned and walked away. I waited in the hallway for him, and I couldn't help but overhear the conversation that took place in his coach's office.

"Coach," he said, his voice wavering almost imperceptibly.

"Hi, Jon. How—what are you doing on crutches?"

Jon told him he'd been in a ski accident, shared the doctor's prognosis.

The coach let out a few swear words. Some that would impress even my father. "How could you be so careless?"

"Coach, I promise I'd never jeopardize track—"

"Can you run?"

Jon paused a beat. "No."

"Then you did, and I don't think there's anything more to say. Bring your uniform and all the gear we gave you by my office tomorrow."

"Coach, I—"

"There's nothing more to say, Jon. You had a nice run."

Well, that just seemed cruel.

Jon's crutches clacked as he adjusted them on the tile. I wondered what he would say next—or if he would just leave.

"And Jon?"

"Yeah?" All hope had left his voice.

"That includes your water bottle."

I didn't even bother clearing my expression before Jon came out. I could have strangled his coach for saying those things to him. Couldn't he tell Jon was hurting? That he was a human being with a life outside of stopwatches and training plans?

"Jon, I'm so sorry," I said.

Crying would have been better than the emotions I saw on his face. Or lack thereof. He'd turned stony, burying everything happening beneath the surface of his smooth features. "I'll see you later."

"But how—"

He shook his head and forced a smile. "I'll be in my dorm. Swing by when you're done."

I stood in the hallway, adrift, as my rock crumbled and walked away from me.

My eyes landed on the office, on the person

who'd been so cold and callous to Jon. Couldn't he tell Jon was devastated? Lost?

The more I thought about it, the angrier I got. The guy might have been a collegiate track coach, but the athletes he worked with had real life feelings.

Before I knew what I was doing, I was standing in his office, shaking with rage. "How dare you," I whispered.

He looked up at me, folded his arms. "Abi, what are you doing here?"

"He came to you, told you the truth, like a man, and all you could do was dismiss him like he's worthless to you?"

"He is," the coach said, as unfeeling as the tile floor beneath us. "He can't run on my team. As an athlete, I can't use him anymore."

"He's more than a pair of legs," I argued, my voice rising higher. "He's kind and funny and smart, and he's overcome more than you could possibly imagine. For you to write him off like that is more than rude. It's cruel."

He raised an eyebrow. "Your point?"

"Eat shit." I spun and left his office.

I knew this would get back to Coach Cadence, but I didn't care. If this was college athletics, I didn't want any part in it.

I went to the training center and sat beside Nikki, who was casually stretching her hamstrings.

"What happened to Jon?" she asked. "I saw him on crutches."

"It's a long story," I said and filled her in. Including the confrontation I'd had with his coach. My voice was still shaking as I laid the final words on her.

Nikki's eyes widened. "You said that?"

I nodded, my cheeks heating. I shouldn't have used that phrase. Even if it was how I felt.

She nudged my shoulder. "Girl, I knew you had some fire in you."

"Yeah." I rolled my eyes. "Just enough to get me burned. Cadence is going to kick me off the team when she hears."

"No way," she said. "You're doing well, and we need you for the points. Plus, Coach Rawlins is a hothead. He'll respect you for standing up to him."

"I don't need his respect," I seethed. "I need him to treat people better."

"I'm sorry that happened to Jon." She frowned at the floor. "I can't imagine how scary it must have been."

I blinked back the image of Jon lying in the snow,

blood pooling beneath him, not knowing whether he would be okay or not. "It was horrible," I breathed.

"Ladies," Coach Cadence called from behind us. "Get started with warm-up. Abi, come here."

Nikki and I exchanged glances.

"Say a prayer for me," I muttered.

"You'll be fine," she reassured.

As she began warming up with the team, I walked to Coach Cadence with my head held high, ready to defend myself and Jon.

She turned away from the others and lowered her voice. "Abi, Coach Rawlins just spoke with me."

I swallowed, nodded.

"I'm so sorry about Jon. Is there anything I can do?"

I blinked, stunned. "I'm not in trouble?"

"No." She chuckled. "But make cursing at coaches a habit, and you might be."

My shoulders finally relaxed. "I don't think there's anything you can do. It's just..." I tried to gauge how much I should tell her. "Running was Jon's life. I don't know what he's going to do without it."

She nodded like she completely understood. "It will be hard, but he's going to have to find something new to focus on. Something healthy. If he can do that, he'll be okay. If not..."

Even without the rest of the sentence, I knew. He'd spiral.

I promised myself to help him find his new passion. To find himself outside of white lines and tennis shoes.

"Now, go warm up," Coach said. "We've got a meet coming up, and we need you."

As I ran toward the rest of the team, I tried to bury my guilt that I was here, living Jon's dream, while he was alone in the dorms, living his nightmare.

CHAPTER THIRTY

WHEN I GOT BACK to the dorms after practice, I knocked on Jon's door, but he didn't answer. I figured he went somewhere or was taking a nap, so I sent him a text asking him to let me know when he wanted to hang out. Then I went back to my room.

What did I do now? It was freezing outside, Anika was still in Roderdale, Jon was tied up with something. A thought popped in my mind.

I messaged Nikki.

Abi: Help.

Abi: So. Bored.

Plus, I didn't like being alone anymore. But I didn't need to make myself sound entirely pathetic by sending that and letting her know.

Nikki: Come outside in ten. I have an idea.

I pocketed my phone, threw on a coat, and headed downstairs. Priscilla waited out front, exhaust pouring from her tailpipe.

When I'd gotten in and closed the door behind me, I said, "This thing is an environmental nightmare."

She patted the dash and leaned close to the steering wheel. "Shh, Priscilla, it's okay. Abi didn't mean it."

I shoved her shoulder, laughing. With a smile on her own face, she put the pickup into drive and started across town.

"What's the plan?" I asked.

"Ever been ice skating?"

"Ever been to the moon?"

She chuckled. "So I take that as a no?"

"Nope. And the thought of busting my butt on ice doesn't exactly sound fun."

"Girl, you'll be fine. Hug the wall if you need to."

I pretended I was hugging her pickup.

"Not now!" she cried, laughing.

I joined in her laughter. Hanging out with Nikki felt so light and freeing after my time at home. With Jon, a small, unwilling part of me admitted.

I needed this.

My phone went off with a new message.

Jon: Hey, sorry, I was taking a shower. Are you not in your room?

Abi: It's fine. I'm hanging out with Nikki.

Jon: Oh.

Abi: Is that okay?

Jon: I guess. I just thought we were going to spend some time together.

Abi: Later. I promise.

Jon: Sure.

Abi: I love you. Talk to you soon.

Jon: Bye.

I frowned at my phone. I knew you couldn't really hear tone in text messages, but Jon seemed disappointed. Why hadn't he said he loved me back?

"What's going on?" Nikki asked, glancing over from the road.

I shook my head. "Jon's been...I don't know. He's off."

"I'm sure he's just having a hard time adjusting. I have no idea what I'd do if I couldn't run anymore."

I nodded, but it was more than that. This was the second time he'd acted upset about me hanging out with my friends. I knew he needed me, but I needed time to myself too.

What was I thinking? Jon wasn't possessive. He was probably just surprised. And lonely, like I felt when he wasn't around. Wasn't that why I'd reached out to Nikki? Plus, we had planned to spend the afternoon together. As more guilt settled over me, I sent him another message.

Abi: Let's grab supper tonight.

Jon replied a few minutes later.

Jon: Can't wait. Love you too.

Feeling a little better, I put my phone in my purse.

Nikki turned up the radio. "I love this song!"

I'd heard it a few times. Enough to sing along and completely butcher the lyrics.

"Stop!" Nikki cried. "You're ruining it!"

I sang another line even louder.

"She does *not* say 'pigs eat men from broken down!'" Nikki yelled through tears of laughter.

I laughed with her as she pulled into the ice rink parking lot and turned off her pickup, effectively cutting off the song.

"What?" I asked innocently. "You didn't want to listen to the rest of the song? I was just getting into it."

She rolled her eyes. "Come on, Ms. Underwood, let's get inside."

After checking out ice skates and putting them on, we wobbled over to the ice. Nikki was a natural athlete, making her way better at ice skating than me. It probably helped that she'd practiced a few times before. She easily glided over the ice, her hands linked behind her back.

I, however, clung to the wall (as suggested) and had no intentions of letting go any time soon.

She made a loop by me and slid to an easy stop. "How's it going, girl?"

"I hate you."

"That good?"

I shook my head, exasperated, and started shuffling toward the exit. "I'm getting some cocoa."

"I'm going to make a few more turns. Grab me some?"

"Sure." Somehow, I made it to the edge and tossed off my skates, walking in my snowflake socks to the concession stand.

As I sat on one of the benches, watching the couples skating together, holding hands, I couldn't help the ache of jealousy that formed in the pit of my stomach. Never mind that I could hardly stay upright, that could have been Jon and me. But I had to remove that possibility from my mind. At least in the near future. We both had bigger things to worry about.

On the way home, Jon texted me a screen shot of a reservation confirmation at a restaurant.

Jon: Wear something nice. I'll pick you up at 7.

"Have you ever been to this place?" I asked Nikki, sounding out the Italian name.

Her eyes widened. "He's taking you there?"

"What?" I asked. "Is it bad?"

She shook her head quickly. "No, it's just—is he proposing? It's super fancy there."

My brows came together. Proposing? "I don't think so. I don't know why he would right now. It's not exactly great timing."

One of her shoulders lifted. "You never know. I mean, you do have mad ice-skating skills. I wouldn't blame him for not being able to wait."

"You suck."

She laughed. "You'll like it. It's a really pretty restaurant. My parents took me there after I signed for the track team. You can see the entire city from there."

My mind flashed back to the library tower, to the guy who'd stood beside me, a wolf in sheep's clothing. How could I have known who Eric was? That he had a vendetta against my dad that made me guilty by association?

"You look like you've seen a ghost. Do you not want him to propose?" she asked.

I shook my head, trying to focus on the moment. "No, it's not that. I mean, I want to marry him someday. I'm just…" I sighed at my inability to string a complete thought together. "It's been a long couple of weeks."

She reached over and rubbed my back. "I'm here for you, girl."

I smiled. "Don't let Priscilla hear that."

Even though I tried to act cavalier, I couldn't shake Nikki's first question. Was Jon proposing? And then her second. Did I want him to?

CHAPTER THIRTY-ONE

THERE WAS no amount of make-up or weight loss
or skin-smoothing girdles that would ever make me
feel comfortable in a dress. Much less this strappy
one Grandma had insisted I buy for special occa-
sions. I couldn't even wear a bra with the thing.
The pink silk slid over my skin and revealed every
curve of my body—even the ones I didn't like so
much. Thin ribbons of fabric criss-crossed over my
back, revealing skin almost all the way down to my
waist.

As I turned from the mirror, I knew my brain
was still trying to reconcile my old appearance with
my new one. My therapist had taught me that, at
least. To turn away and focus on what I knew to be
true.

Right now, I knew Jon would be here any second. And I hoped he wouldn't be disappointed.

A knock sounded on my door, and I glanced at the time on my phone. Exactly seven o'clock. How was he always so punctual?

"One second," I called and bent toward my mirror to apply lipstick. I opted for a darker shade that wouldn't compete with my dress.

When I opened the door, his eyes widened.

I gripped my shawl tighter, looking down at the dress. "Is it too much? I can change."

"No, no no." He took my hand and pulled me to him. "You look amazing."

I looped my arms around him, through the gap between his crutches and his sides, and put my chin on his chest. "You don't look so bad yourself."

His eyes sparkled, a light returning that I'd missed seeing there. Part of me hoped he was proposing tonight, just so I could seal forever with him.

I tilted my chin up and kissed him deeply, not worrying about my lipstick or that we were standing in the doorway where anyone in the hall could see. This was Jon. I would never get tired of kissing him. Never be afraid to show anyone else how much I loved him. How happy I was to have him in my life.

His voice was husky as he breathed, "Keep this up, and we won't make it to the restaurant."

By the heaviness of his eyelids and the heat in his breath, I knew he was telling the truth.

It had been a while, which I was feeling pretty intensely right about now. I barely managed to tear myself apart from him and grab my clutch from my desk. "Let's go."

We walked down to his car, and I drove us using directions he pulled up on his phone. The map led us to a tall building in downtown Austin. We rode an elevator up more than twenty floors and then stepped onto a beautiful patio.

Heat radiated from torches stationed throughout the area, and delicate flowers and votive candles rested on each table. But the most amazing thing was the view. My eyes drank in the city, the lights sparkling all around like a bed of stars shining just for us.

"It's stunning," I breathed.

He rested his hand on a bare patch of skin above my waist. "It's all for you."

A smile touched my lips. For a second, I pretended he'd lit the city, individually touched every light so I could have this moment. "I love you," I said and pressed my lips to his.

He smiled against my kiss. "I love you more."

I shook my head, knowing there was no way that was true.

A waiter came and sat us at a table for two, and I was so enthralled with the beautiful table setting and the sights around us, I barely managed to take in the menu. It didn't have prices, which probably was a good thing, because there was no way I'd let Jon spend too much money on me.

Someone took our orders and menus, and then Jon put his hands on the table, palms up. An invitation.

I rested my hands on his, loving the feel of him, of us. "What's all this for?" I asked.

He shrugged, a small smile on his lips.

"Really," I said, short of breath. Was I ready for a proposal? Did I want that? I still didn't know.

He glanced back over the city. "I had to let you know, even though I can't run track, and I won't be going to nationals, and I'm not...good at anything anymore..." His eyes met mine again, the candlelight flickering in his pupils. "I still want to give you the world."

If only he knew he already had. It was sitting right in front of me.

CHAPTER THIRTY-TWO

I WALKED into my dorm after track practice, expecting to find emptiness but seeing something else instead. "What are you two doing here?"

Jon sat in my desk chair while Anika lay on her stomach on the rug, her laptop in front of her.

She laughed, getting to her knees. "Good to see you too."

I went to her and crouched to hug her, even though my legs protested.

Then I caught sight of what Jon held in his hands. "Is that...are you cross-stitching?"

His cheeks went red as he set it down. "I've applied for every job I could find and my mom sent it and I'm bored and—" at Anika's laughter, he said, "sue me," and picked it back up.

Anika and I exchanged glances.

"Abi," she said, standing up, "you have to see this sink in the girls' bathroom. Someone left a fish in there."

"It's alive?" I asked.

She nodded.

"But it's just a goldfish," Jon quipped. "They could have left something cooler."

I dropped my drawstring bag by the bed and said, "Show me."

The second we got out of the dorm, she whispered, "What happened? Jon wouldn't tell me anything."

"What?"

She shook her head. "Just that he got hurt skiing and then he asked me so many questions about my break, I couldn't get any information out of him."

"Figures." I lifted a corner of my lips in a sad smile. He was deflecting. I relayed the whole horrible event to her, and her eyes were wide as she pushed the community bathroom door open.

"Is there really a fish?" I asked.

"Yeah." She led me around to a sink, and sure enough, there was a tiny goldfish with a feeding chart written on the mirror in lipstick. His name was written in big, bold letters across the top.

Cletus

"Terrible name for a fish," Anika muttered.

I nodded, lost in thought. The fish reminded me of the Einstein quote Mr. Pelosi shared with me. "Everyone is a genius. But if you judge a fish by its ability to climb a tree, it will live its whole life believing that it is stupid."

Jon was the fish right now, judging his life on the ability to run. The problem was the measures he'd always used to judge himself weren't applicable anymore. Would he realize that? My eyes misted over, and when blinking away the moisture didn't cut it, I wiped at them.

Anika put an arm around me and rested her head on my shoulder for a second. "I'm sorry break was hard."

All I had left in me was a nod before we turned and walked back to my own beautiful, broken fish.

Jon was terrible at cross-stitching. But I was now the semi-proud owner of a messy cross-stitched heart.

Thank God classes were starting.

Even though Jon didn't have anywhere to be until ten, he got up early and walked across campus with me to my first class—a course called Comparative Politics I couldn't wait to start. When we reached the stairs at the building's entrance, I stopped for our goodbye.

Jon went to the handrail, though, and started up. "I'm walking you to the door."

"This is ridiculous," I said, following him up the stairs. I had to make myself slow down as to not outpace him. "You didn't need to come with me across campus, and you definitely don't need to take all these stairs."

"If you didn't want me to come, you could have said so," he grumbled. "But it's not like I have anything else going on. I'm bored out of my skull."

I softened, feeling sorry for him. I should have realized this was as much for him as it was for me. "What are you going to do until class?" I asked as we topped the stairs.

He lifted one shoulder. "I don't know. Maybe grab a coffee."

"You keep drinking four-dollar lattes, and your parents are going to cut you off."

His expression tightened. "If one of those jobs would call me back, I would be able to pay for it myself."

"You'll hear back," I reassured him.

He refused to look me in the eyes. "You don't know that. I have no experience. No skills. No physical ability to do anything. I doubt I'm at the top of anyone's list."

I frowned. When he got like this, I couldn't argue with him. I just stayed quiet until we reached the classroom, then lifted to my tiptoes and kissed his cheek. "I'll see you after practice tonight."

"We're not getting lunch?"

"I have therapy, remember?"

He looked off to the side. "Guess I forgot."

I picked at the end of my backpack strap, trying to decide whether I should bring it up again or not. I decided to go for it. "You know, you could come with me and set up an appointment. I'm sure it would help."

"Abi, we talked about this. I don't need a shrink. I need a job."

The hourly bell rang, punctuating his point.

I shook my head. "I've got to go to class. I'll see you later."

"Bye," he said, clearly frustrated.

We walked our separate ways, and the ache in my chest only grew.

CHAPTER THIRTY-THREE

"I DON'T KNOW what to do," I admitted to my therapist in session after spending the first half hour telling her about break and all its tragedies. "He's irritable, bored, and he has no drive anymore. It's like he lost all of his purpose, but I don't know why. It wasn't like track was the game plan anyway. He wanted to be a social worker. Now, it seems like all that matters is his injury."

Her dark eyes glanced from her notebook to me. "I can't diagnose him without seeing him, but it sounds like he's depressed."

"He is!" I cried, causing her to scribble in her notebook. I looked down at my hands, trying to get my emotions in check, but that only made speaking over the growing knot in my chest even harder. "I thought the first day was hard, when he got hurt and I had to sit with him as he cried over not being able to run. His whole body shook. And then I thought it was hard when his pain medicine wore off the first time and I heard him, *screaming* out with pain. I thought it was hard when he suffered through physical therapy for the first time." My throat got tight. "But this, watching him lose himself." I swallowed. "It's worse than all of that. It feels like I've lost him too."

My chest heaved with the weight of my cries and both of our losses. "Why am I crying?" I asked. "It's not like it's happening to me. I should just be able to support him, but I-I..." I couldn't bring myself to say the word "can't," even though my lips ached to.

"Abi," she said. "You've been through so much this year. The fact that you're sitting in front of me, cohesively stating your emotions and needs is nothing short of a miracle." She glanced at the clock. "And you've spent almost the whole hour trying to help someone else with their needs. What about you? Are you still having flashbacks? Nightmares?"

I blinked. Me? I hadn't thought of myself in weeks. Slowly, I shook my head. "I've been so wrapped up in Jon..."

Her smile was soft. "Don't let your healing get pushed to the back burner. It matters too."

She made me promise to practice self-care after our session, but I didn't need her extra push. Therapy always wore me out. I left feeling like I'd been run over by a truck, my eyes stinging and skin raw from the deluge of tears that accompanied my sessions without fail. I walked back to my dorm with my hood up and earphones in, praying I wouldn't run into anyone, but also not wanting to be alone.

Anika was a welcome sight in the dorm, sitting in front of her desk.

"Hey." She smiled up at me, then her expression sobered as she took me in. "Therapy day?"

I nodded, shrugging off my coat.

"Sorry," she said and paused. "Want to watch some *Sex and the City*? It always cheers me up."

"What?" I asked. "What's *Sex in the City*? It sounds like a porno."

Her laughter was almost contagious. "*Sex and the City*. It makes me feel better, you know if I've had a long day or got a bad grade or—"

"I know what you said; I just don't know what you're talking about," I elaborated.

Anika's hands froze on her paper as she stared at

me open-mouthed. "No. Freaking. Way. Miranda? Carrie?"

"Brandy? Tiffany?" I half-heartedly teased.

She pretended to pull at her hair in exasperation. "Where have you been living?"

"Under a rock, apparently."

"Right?" She went to get the remote and then crawled into her bunk. "You've got to see this. It doesn't get really good until season two, but you need the backstory."

Thankful for a distraction, I climbed into my own bed. "Please, keep talking." I meant that whole-heartedly.

Anika talked me through the first three episodes until I was finally relaxed enough to drift off to sleep, curled under my blankets.

When I woke up, there were a few text messages and a string of new emails waiting in my notifications. All from Jon.

Sex and the City still played on the TV, even though Anika was gone, a note on her desk. Probably saying she was at the library. That girl studied like crazy.

I looked down at my phone, reading my texts.

Jon: Call me?

Jon: Are you okay?

I hit dial on my phone and scrolled through my emails as it rang. Jon had forwarded me rejection letter after rejection letter from all of his job applications. My heart hurt for him, at how cast-off he must have been feeling.

"Hello? Are you okay?" he asked.

"I'm fine," I said. "Just fell asleep after my appointment. It sounds like you've had a rough day."

"A rough day is losing ten dollars. A rough day is stepping in a pile of dog poo. This is...well, worse than that."

I could relate. "So, you're okay?"

"If okay means completely unemployable, then yes."

"This can't be everywhere you've applied," I pointed out. "When I was looking for jobs in Woodman, it took me forever to get answers. I'm probably still getting rejection emails."

"It's not everywhere." He sighed. "But the odds aren't looking good."

I sat up on my bed, rubbing the sleep from my eyes. "Look, you don't need everyone to like you."

"What's that supposed to mean?" A defensive edge colored his voice.

I back-pedalled so fast I could practically feel my toes scraping my throat. "It just means that you only need one person to hire you. Right? You're just looking for one job?"

He let out another sigh. "Right. But it would be nice to have options."

"Yeah." I shrugged. "And a million dollars."

"And someone up here to cuddle with."

I smiled for the first time in our whole conversation. "I might be able to arrange that."

"Yeah?"

"Yep." I pulled my blanket back and started crawling down from bed. "I'll have my people call your people."

"And by that you mean?"

"I'll be there in five."

CHAPTER THIRTY-FOUR

AROUND NINE, I woke to a call from my grandma.

Jon rolled over in bed, half-asleep. "Send it to voicemail."

"That's okay." I hit silence and kissed his cheek. "I need to go back to my room anyway."

He mumbled out those three special words, "I love you," and was snoring before it rang again. I climbed out of his bed, slipped on my shoes, and got to the hallway before returning Grandma's call.

"You called me back." The way she said it almost made it seem like she was disappointed.

"Why wouldn't I?" I ventured.

Grandma was quiet for a moment. I pictured her rubbing her temples, her eyes closed.

Each of my senses went on high alert, and I paused in the hallway. "What's going on?"

"Abi, I have good news and bad news."

My heart sped. In my situation, you'd take anything you could. "Good news."

"Eric Shepherd took a plea bargain. He's serving a twenty-five-year sentence in a maximum-security prison."

I staggered back and leaned against the wall. I almost didn't know how I should feel. Relieved I wouldn't have to see Eric face to face? Scared of what would happen after year twenty-five? Angry he didn't get more time? But I knew deep down the person who deserved to pay most was my father. He'd earned every day of his sentence and more.

"Abi?" she said softly.

"Mm?"

"That's good news, right? No trial?"

"I guess," I said. And maybe it was. I would be nearly fifty years old before Eric got out of prison. Would likely have children and maybe grandchildren and marriage anniversaries into the double digits. But something kept me from celebrating. "The bad news?"

Grandma let out a heavy sigh. "They set your father's parole hearing for a month from today."

The floor dropped out from under me, and I was falling, powerless to stop the descent. At least, that's what it felt like. That, and like all the air had been sucked from the room. I slid down against the hallway wall, just trying to keep from passing out.

"Abi?"

I managed to take a breath and clear the fog clouding my eyes. "When did they decide on that?"

The pause before she spoke told me more than words could. She'd been holding on to this for a while now. "Honey, you've had the world on your shoulders for the last few weeks."

Few weeks? "When did you find out?"

"The first day Jon was in the hospital."

I could hardly wrap my mind around it. While Jon was sitting in the hospital, when Glen tried to talk me into dropping out, plans were being made to give my dad a chance at life as a free man. How could this be?

"I spoke with Glen, and he said if you want to make a statement in the hearing, you can submit one via video in his office, or..." She breathed another heavy sigh. Sharing the news was weighing on her as much as receiving it was on me.

"Or what, Gram?"

"You could go to the prison yourself."

I drew my knees to my chest and held my head in my hands. When would this all be over? When would my past stop following me? Why couldn't I be a normal, supportive girlfriend and just focus on my hurting boyfriend?

He was snoring just a few doors down, but I couldn't go to him. Not right now. Not now that he was actually sleeping and feeling good after all the rejection letters and we'd had a good night together. Not just to worry him over something that had apparently been in the works for a while now.

"What are you going to do, Abi?"

I stared at the ceiling, at a water stain that looked like a brown ink blot test. "Can you just tell me what to do?"

"I wish I could." She paused. "It's your choice, but I do think you should say something to him. He shouldn't get the last word in your life."

CHAPTER THIRTY-FIVE

I WAS at Jon's door first thing after practice the next morning. Kyle answered my knock, dressed in shorts and nothing else, running a towel through his hair.

"Hey, Abi." He turned away and started back toward his desk, giving me a view of the back.

All I could say was...wow.

Jon set his laptop to the side and got off the futon. "Okay, time to get your jaw off the floor, Abs." He wasn't joking.

My cheeks immediately heated. "Well, gotta take advantage, right?" I attempted a playful smile between the two guys, who were obviously not my ideal audience.

Kyle's ears went just as red as mine as he hurriedly threw on a shirt.

Jon just shook his head and turned to Kyle. "You steal my girl, you pay." His words were only a little playful.

I took his hand and laced my fingers through his. I hoped he knew no one could compare to him. Not Kyle, not anyone. "Hey, can we talk?"

His eyebrows creased. "Everything okay?"

"I don't know," I admitted.

Kyle grabbed his backpack. "I'm heading to the library to study with Anika. I'll see you two later."

I felt a little bad that he was always rushing out so Jon and I could have privacy. He'd been my boyfriend's roommate and my roommate's boyfriend for more than a semester now, and I felt like I barely knew him. "Hey, are you up for a double date with Jon and me? Anika and I have talked about it a few times, but never made it happen."

He gave me a genuine smile. "That sounds awesome. Saturday?"

"Sure," I said.

Kyle walked out, shutting the door behind him, and when I turned to Jon, I found a sour expression waiting for me.

"What?" he said. "You can just make plans for us now without running them by me?"

My heart sank. "That's not what I meant. I just

know you don't have a lot going on anymore, so..." I stared toward the ceiling. I was just digging myself an even deeper hole.

"I get it." He fell back on the futon, pulling his computer onto his lap. "I'm not on the track team anymore. I don't have a job. I'm a loser with nothing to do."

My eyebrows snapped together. "Jon, you can't think like that."

"Loser" and "Jon" were two words that didn't belong in the same sentence. On the same planet.

His eyes met mine, tortured. "Why not?"

"Because it's the farthest thing from the truth." I went to him and cupped his cheek, rubbed my thumb over the crest of his cheekbone. "I wish you could see what I see in you."

He closed his eyes against my words and took in a shaky breath. "Me too."

I let my hand fall from his cheek as I sat next to him on the futon, pulled his computer away, and curled even closer him. I didn't know what else to do other than be there.

His arms surrounded me, and he held me close like he was clinging on to the very threads that made him who he was.

Eventually, his breathing evened out, and he sat

up. "Did you just come by to hang out?" He said it like he'd just remembered it.

"Oh." My heart constricted even further. I didn't want to trouble him with the word "loser" still echoing around the room. Around my chest. But after last semester, I'd made a promise to be upfront with him. Even if it made me uncomfortable. And my therapist was right. I mattered too.

He stiffened. "What's wrong, Abi?"

"My dad is up for parole, and the hearing is next month."

"Next month?" His mouth went slack.

I nodded.

"That's so soon."

I nodded.

"Are you going?"

Again, I nodded.

He frowned, every thought and emotion flicking unbridled across his visage. "Are you sure?"

"I have to go," I said. "I have to."

"Haven't you been through enough?"

A sardonic laugh escaped my lips. Everyone around me was starting to sound like an echo chamber. Everything that had happened to me, it was enough to fill a lifetime of heartache. But I didn't get to decide that. What I could control was myself, now. "All of the things he's done to me...to Lupita...I have to do what I can to make sure he doesn't walk free again. Not so soon."

Jon rubbed my back in big, slow circles. "Whatever you need, I'm here."

I wanted to believe him. But could he handle being my rock with so much on his own plate? I admitted a truth I didn't want to recognize. "I need you."

I leaned into his warmth, into the rise and fall of his chest and the rhythm of his breaths. Sitting so close to him used to feel like being reset, reminded of what I had. But now I could only remember what I had to lose.

CHAPTER THIRTY-SIX

ANIKA LEANED CLOSER to her compact mirror, wiping at her makeup. "Why is it so impossible to put on matching lines of eyeliner?"

I cringed at my own uneven lines. "There's a reason they focused on the lunar landing first."

She giggled. "Whatever. I'm putting some eyeshadow over it."

"One small step for Anika," I said.

"One giant leap for women everywhere," she finished, laughing. "I'm so excited to double date with you guys. Why the heck has it taken this long?"

The honest answer? "I've been pretty wrapped up in myself."

As I said it, I knew how true it was. I didn't feel guilty or attached to the answer. I'd had enough to worry about just keeping my head above water.

"You've had a lot going on," Anika said, not arguing.

"I know." I smiled, twisting in my chair so she could see I meant my words. "But I'm here for you now, I promise."

She smiled back at me in her mirror. "Back at you."

"Good." I closed my mascara and looked in the mirror. "Tonight's going to be so good for Jon."

Her eyes widened in acknowledgement. "The injury's been tough for him, huh?"

"It's been tough for all of us," I admitted. "I just don't know how to fix it."

"You know you can't," she said. "We can't take away anyone else's pain. We can just make sure they don't suffer alone."

My heart latched on to her words. That was so much easier said than done.

"Is he going to your track meet tomorrow?" she asked, putting her makeup back in her zipper pouch.

I nodded. "Luckily, his parents and my grandma are coming. I wouldn't want him to go alone."

"Can I sit with them?" she asked.

My eyebrows rose. I'd never even thought of

asking Anika to a track meet, but now that football was over for Kyle, it made sense. "I'd love that!"

She smiled. "Me too."

A knock sounded on our door.

"I guess that's our ride," I said, getting up to answer it.

I swung the door open, and I swear, it wasn't fair for both of our boyfriends to be standing in the hall-way, dressed up for a date, side by side. Kyle had traded out his usual sweats and tennis shoes for jeans and cowboy boots with a button-up shirt he filled out all too well. And then Jon. The piece de résistance with a tight navy-blue sweater that brought out the depth in his eyes, jeans that hugged him in all the right places, a gray stocking cap with his dark brown hair sticking out from the bottom. How he had ended up at my door and not at a name-brand photo shoot, I had no idea.

Anika came up behind me and draped my coat over my shoulders. "Ready to go?"

I nodded. The guys nodded. And we left the dorm, locking the door behind us. Kyle casually threw his arm over Anika's shoulder, and they walked ahead of us toward the elevators. A small part of me felt jealous that Jon had to walk on crutches, separated from me.

I tried shaking the feeling with a question. "What's the plan for tonight?"

Anika turned her head and looked back at us over Kyle's arm. "I was thinking karaoke?"

"Fun," I said, which was really translation for *why in the world would we want to engage in such a masochistic display of humiliation in front of an unnamed audience?*

Jon met my eyes. His gaze said the same thing.

I just shrugged. We couldn't say what a terrible idea it was in front of the other two. They knew where we slept.

Kyle had pulled his black pickup up front and had it running with remote start. After he got the doors unlocked, Jon and I climbed into the spacious back seat. While he buckled into the seat by the door, I slid into the middle and belted in so I could sit next to him. I loved going on dates with Jon. Especially ones where we didn't have a center console separating us.

With a twist of the dial, country music poured through the speakers. A song about love and loss and the night sky. I glanced out the window but couldn't spot any stars. Austin was too lit up at night, not like Woodman with its sparse streetlamps. I could always count on a few specks of light there.

Jon squeezed my hand, and I leaned my head on his shoulder. This was nice.

Anika twisted in the front seat and looked back at us. "What song are you going to sing tonight?"

Jon laughed at the same time I did, making Anika draw her eyebrows together.

"We're not musical people," I explained. "And don't even ask to see us dance."

"Even before my injury," Jon added.

Kyle chuckled low. "You don't have to be an expert to hold your girl close and sway around."

Anika smiled at him with gooey eyes. I loved that they loved each other so much. Jealousy ached in me at the fact that they could just enjoy each other and their freshman year of college. I wanted that for Jon and me so badly, but I was starting to wonder if an untroubled day, much less year, would ever happen.

I held Jon's hand just a little tighter. At least we had this moment together. I needed to savor it.

Kyle pulled in front of a bar and stopped along the sidewalk. "I'll let you off here, Jon."

"I can walk," Jon said. "Go ahead."

"It's no problem, man."

"That's a good idea," I agreed. "We can wait for them up front."

Jon's voice got tight. "I said, 'Go ahead.'"

My heart recoiled, and Kyle glanced at us in the rear-view mirror, his eyes showing the surprise I felt at the force behind Jon's statement. But no one uttered another word contrary. Kyle put the pickup in drive. We had to park at least a quarter of a mile away, and Jon leaned heavily on his crutches for the long walk.

There wasn't enough room for him and me and the other people walking by on the sidewalk, so I had to walk behind him, in a single-file line, watching his shoulders labor with each swing of his crutches and brace.

Anika and Kyle walked ahead, in their own world, and I found myself wishing I could be in my own world too. Why hadn't Jon just accepted the offer? It was nice, thoughtful, of Kyle to think of dropping us off closer.

By the time we reached the club, Jon's face was tight with pain. Walking on the crutches hurt his underarms, and putting so much pressure on one of his legs wasn't healthy.

As if that weren't bad enough, all of the seats were full inside the bar, leaving us leaning against a wall instead of resting like Jon needed to be.

"I'm going to sign us up for a song," Anika said to me. "Are you good with 'Tuxedo'?"

"First of all, if it's a country song, no," I quipped. "And I don't sing, so... also, no."

She laughed. "It'll be fun. I promise." And then she turned and disappeared toward the DJ stand.

"Did you put her up to this?" I asked Jon.

He managed a smile that didn't quite reach his eyes. "No, but I should have."

"Have you heard the song?"

He sang a few painfully cringy, twangy lines from a song about men with strong hands.

"God no."

"Yes, ma'am."

I flinched. "Be sure to remove all the evidence."

"It might cost you something," he said over the current drunken pair singing "Friends in Low Places."

"What's that?" I asked.

His eyes sizzled. "I think you know."

"Oh?" Fire lit in the pit of my stomach, melting the ice that had been there earlier.

He nodded. "Think you can handle it?"

I stepped closer to him, raised myself on my tiptoes, and whispered, "Yes." It had been way too long. To seal the deal, I nibbled his earlobe.

He gasped, gripping my side, but I pulled back.

"Just a preview," I said, winking.

"Can't wait for the real thing." There was no humor in his voice. Only the real hunger I felt growing inside me.

"Can we just go home?" I asked.

He nodded over my shoulder. "I don't think Anika would let that happen."

"What?"

I turned just in time to see Anika yell from the stage, "We're up!"

CHAPTER THIRTY-SEVEN

OF ALL THE forms of torture in the world,
standing in front of a room packed with people,
including my smirking boyfriend, had to lead the list
for top ten worst.

Anika handed me a microphone, her eyes gleaming. I stared at the sign in front of us that said dropping the microphone would result in a hundred-
dollar fine.

I wanted to tell them no one was going to be
performing well enough to warrant a mic drop.

Well, except maybe Anika, who was rocking
back and forth to the opening chords of the music.

"Are you drunk?" I asked her, away from my mic.
She had to be drunk to do this on purpose.

Laughing, she shook her head and pointed at the screen with words on it. "Let's go!"

She sang the opening lines of the song, her voice perfectly hitting each note, and the crowd cheered for her.

Her eyes told me to join. So I did. Badly.

I covered my face, then peeked out to catch Jon sniggering, whooping for us. Honestly, I'd make a fool out of myself every day of the week to see him having this much fun. So I hammed it up. Did my best awkward country two-step on the stage, hooked my fingers in my belt loops, twirled hair around my finger, sang with Anika like the song was made for us to perform.

At the end, the crowd had their hands in the air. Anika set the mic in the stand. "One, two, three, cannonball!" She flung herself into the crowd, who lifted her up.

Jon raised an eyebrow at me, and all of a sudden I was in the cemetery again, staring into Roberto's coal-black sparkling eyes as he dared me to go streaking with the rest of them. And I was saying I wanted to live.

I took a running start and leapt into the hands of the people who passed me along with Anika. I caught sight of her grin and beamed right along with her. This was what college should be like. Pure euphoria. Singing horribly to a crowd who loved it anyway. My boyfriend laughing and having the time of his life.

The hands passed us to the back of the room, and a couple of guys made sure Anika and I landed on our feet. They were cute, big, not fit, but strong —clearly.

"Want a drink?" the one closest to Anika asked.

"We're not allowed," I said at the same time Anika said, "We have boyfriends!"

Her answer was way smoother than mine. Either way, the guys left, and we worked our way back toward our guys, who had finally found an open booth.

Jon moved his brace out of the way and opened his arms for me. "There's my Mariah Carey!"

I rolled my eyes, blushing harder than before. "I prefer Shakira."

"Your hips don't lie." He smirked.

I kissed the smirk right off his face, still high with the rush of performing, crowd-surfing, and his smile, wider than I'd seen it in weeks. "I love you," I said.

"I love you more."

"I'll remember you when I make it big."

He pulled me in closer and smiled over at Anika. "You have a voice."

Kyle grinned proudly. "She's amazing. I've been getting her to sing at church."

Anika buried her head in his shoulder, bashful yet again, like all that confidence I'd seen on stage was just a show.

Jon lifted his chin. "Do you practice the crowd-surfing there too?"

"God no," she said.

Jon got out his phone and swiped to a photo of the two of us lifted high in the air. "You sure?" He held it out to her. "You look right at home."

"Please." She took a drink of Kyle's pop and kept her eyes on the cup.

A new song came on, and Kyle asked her to dance. As he led her to the dance floor, I snuggled in closer to Jon.

"Kyle was right about one thing," Jon said. "I'll never need an excuse to hold you close."

CHAPTER THIRTY-EIGHT

THE NEXT MORNING, I ate breakfast with Jon, Anika, and Kyle. They were all planning on going to my track meet together and getting together our families there.

Nervous flutters filled my stomach. First that my friends would be watching me run for the first time. Second that I would encounter someone who'd seen my spectacle from the night before. What the hell had gotten into me?

Then I looked across the table at Jon. At his green eyes and the short stubble on his chin, at the curve of his lips, and I remembered why I'd made such a fool of myself.

He was in full-blown cheery mode this morning, trying to pretend the fact that this would be the first track meet for him off the team wasn't eating him alive inside.

I reached across the table for his hand, and he took it, but he wouldn't meet my eyes. He didn't want to be comforted right now. So, I did what Anika suggested—sat with him through his pain.

But I couldn't sit with him forever.

"I better get going," I said, trying to gauge his reaction.

His face was a clear slate. "Good luck, babe. You're gonna do great."

"Are you okay?" I asked low. Anika and Kyle could probably hear, but I meant it just for him.

"I'm fine," he said just as loud as before. Like he wanted them to know he wasn't suffering. "Now, focus on you. Don't worry about me."

"Can't help it," I admitted.

"Look, Abs," he said, finally meeting my eyes. "Don't waste it, okay?"

I nodded and stood up to leave. The fact was Jon had been the one in love with running and competing. I was just fine making the loop around our neighborhood in the morning. If college track wasn't paying for my degree, I would happily trade the early mornings and extra travel for more study time or a nap here and there.

But this was my situation, and I promised I'd make the most of it for Jon. I went back to my room, changed into my uniform, and walked to the training center where the team was meeting for warm-up.

Since it was a home meet, we got the advantage of preparing for the day here instead of a different field the hosting university offered.

I took a seat on the ground beside Nikki and started stretching.

"How's Jon doing?" she asked.

I shrugged, trying not to show how upset I was for him. It almost would have been better if he'd cried or broken down or done anything except put on the act that he had. At least then I'd have some idea of what to do to help him.

She nodded. "I couldn't imagine not running."

That was the problem. I could. "I'd do anything to trade places with him."

I knew it was wishful thinking, and that didn't get me anywhere good. Nikki must have known that because she simply stayed beside me, preparing for the meet, showing me I wasn't alone.

Coach Cadence called the group together, and when we'd circled her, she began. "Ladies, we've been working hard. We're getting closer and closer to the indoor nationals, and I want you to run every single race like it's for the national title. Do you understand?"

We nodded. She'd been running us in practices like the gold depended on it. Because it did. I knew I wouldn't get anywhere near the platform, but the other girls were competitive, especially Nikki and Mollie.

We left the training center and went about the meet as usual. Except this time, I couldn't watch Jon race, couldn't see his confidence and attempt to absorb it. Instead, as I stood at the starting line about to begin my race, I looked to the stands, searching for him. For some hint everything was okay.

Jon was walking away from the track, up the bleacher stairs.

The starting gun went off, and I jumped, unprepared.

I heard Coach Cadence yell, "GET YOUR HEAD IN THE RACE, JOHNSON."

And I did, more out of survival than anything. Jon, my rock, was walking away. It was too painful for him to see me running. So as I put one foot in front of the other, trying to maintain my middle-of-the-pack status, the love of my life was suffering alone.

I ran a terrible race, securing my worst time of

the season. Coach Cadence barely hid her disappointment in the firm set of her lips, saying she'd talk to me at practice Monday.

Refusing to make eye contact with my teammates, I went to the locker room to shower up and meet my family.

They waited for me where I'd seen them in the stands, Anika and Kyle included, but I didn't see the one person I really wanted to.

Grandma answered the question in my eyes. "Jon said his leg was hurting, hon. Went to the dorms to lie down."

Anika came forward and gave me a big hug. "That was amazing, Abi. I had no idea you could run like that!"

My lips twitched, not quite able to form a smile. "Thanks, girl."

As she stepped back, Kyle came forward, his hand in the air for a high-five.

After I slapped his hand, he said, "We better get going, but good job today!"

I smiled, thanked him, and went to Grandma, who wrapped her arm around me. I rested my head on her thin shoulder. She reached up and patted my cheek with her hand. The Scollers watched our exchange, at a loss.

What could they say? Jon was their son. The situation sucked all around. There was no other word for how much it sucked.

"Do you want to get dinner?" Grandma asked.

I wiped at my eyes. "I actually have a headache. Would you be upset if I just went back to the dorms?"

Her eyes told me she saw right through me, but still, she said, "Not at all, sweetie. Take care of yourself." A reminder.

I nodded. "I will."

Marta and Glen said goodbye, gave me long hugs each, and then they left. They'd offered me a ride to the dorm, but I wanted to walk. Clear my head. Maybe this frigid January air would do me some good.

Plus, I knew what I was going to face when I found Jon would be harder than walking in below-freezing temperatures. I needed time to prepare for what would come next.

CHAPTER THIRTY-NINE

I PUSHED OPEN the door to Jon's room, and he let out an exaggerated, fake yawn. If he thought he was fooling me, he was wrong. I knew his real yawns—had fallen asleep beside him and woken up in the same place enough to tell.

"What happened back there?" I asked, standing at his bed, almost at eye level.

His eyes were sharp, just more proof he'd been awake. "My leg was hurting so bad. I came back to get some medicine and take a nap."

"Are you feeling better? Emotionally?" I asked.

"What do you mean?"

I tilted my head, pressing my lips together. "It was probably hard going to the track meet. I know that."

"It wasn't." He flung back his comforter, still fully dressed, and sat up, rubbing his hair. "My leg was hurting because a ski pole lodged itself in my thigh while I was trying to teach you to snowboard, if you don't remember."

I recoiled from the slap of his words. "Of course I remember. I sat by you in the hospital for a week!"

"Then I don't know why you're acting like I'm not hurt." He carefully climbed down the ladder and then went to his desk, beginning the steps to strap on his brace.

"I'm not," I said. "I just..." I looked over my shoulder, out the dorm window. At all the people with normal, happy lives passing below. "I'm worried about you."

"Don't be." His eyes stayed trained on the straps of his brace. "Actually, I'm so fine, and the medicine helped so much, that I wanted to ask you to a party. Some guys from my lit class are having one at their house tonight."

I eyed him. "A house party?" He'd steered so clear of those our first semester, they might as well have been marked with caution, active contagion, people-named-Jon-don't-come-near-here tape.

"Yep." He popped the p. "You game?"

I couldn't believe this. "Are you sure you're okay?"

He nodded, forcing a smile. "If I was any more okay, I'd have to change my name to Oscar Kangaroo. Get it? O. K.?"

"What about CK? Crazy Kangaroo?"

He shrugged. "Has a nice ring to it, don't you think?"

I rolled my eyes. "What time is it?"

"Four."

"No, I meant the party?"

"Oh, whenever. Thought we could head over around ten?"

"Sure." I rubbed my arm. "I guess...I'll see you then?"

"You don't want to stay and hang out?"

I shook my head, and at his fallen features, I said, "I mean, I do, but I need a nap and to get some studying in."

As he rubbed his hand over the back of his neck and nodded, he looked completely lost. The problem was, I didn't think I was the one who could help him find his way.

* * *

Around nine, my phone started ringing. I dug it from under my blankets and saw Stormy's name on the screen, requesting a video call. "Hello?"

She grinned at me from her car, the overhead lights patchily illuminating her face. "You are a beast!"

I leaned back against the wall, my eyebrows creased. "What?"

"I streamed your race before my shift! I got to see you run!"

Heat immediately found my face. Of all my track meets so far, this was the last one I would have wanted her to see.

"What?" she asked, buckling up. "Did you freeze?"

"I'm here," I said. "I can't believe you watched it."

"I had to do something. I was so bored." She groaned. "I've been having Braxton Hicks, and whenever Frank's home, he puts me on bed rest!"

"Braxton Hicks? Is that a band?"

She laughed. "No, it's like, fake contractions."

"You still have two months 'til your due date, though." I sat up, on edge. "Why're you having contractions? Are you okay?"

"God, you're just as bad as Frank." She rolled her

head to the side, leaning against the window. "They're normal. And a pain in the ass."

I shook my head, smiling. Pregnancy definitely hadn't changed Stormy's spirit.

"How'd Jon do?" she asked.

I frowned.

"That bad?"

"Let's just say he left before my race even started."

She cringed. "Ouch."

"Yeah. And then he got all defensive when I asked him about it."

"Guys." She rolled her eyes. "Anytime I even mention Frank might be a *little* scared about being a dad, he loses it."

"How's he doing?"

She shrugged. "I mean, good. Doting." She smiled. "Terrified, even if he doesn't want to admit it."

"If he's going to be in the delivery room with you, he should be."

"You're so lucky I'm not there. I totally would have hit you." She laughed. "But, really, there was something I wanted to ask."

"What's up?"

"Will you be there with me? When I have the baby?"

My mouth fell open. Then closed.

"It's okay if you don't want to," she rushed out.

"No!" I said, shaking my head too fast. "No, it's not that, it's just, are you sure?"

With her lips in a tight smile, she nodded. "I can have two people. One will be Frank, and the other spot is yours... If you want it."

"Of course. I'll be there," I promised.

CHAPTER FORTY

JON KNOCKED on my door at half past nine.
When I opened it, he stepped in, looking at Anika's
noticeably empty and made bed. "Where'd she go?"

"To visit one of her friends," I said. "She's gone
'til Monday."

Jon tilted his head. "Yeah?"

"Yeah." I sat back at my desk and continued
applying mascara.

He stepped behind me, swept my hair aside, and
placed a kiss on the back of my neck.

My hand froze on the mascara wand as shivers
spread down my spine. "You're going to make me
smudge."

He reached over and grabbed my makeup, dropping it on the desk. "I don't care."

My stomach swooped at the heat in his eyes, at the way he bit his bottom lip. "Oh really?" It came out all breathy, but Jon didn't seem to notice.

His mouth was on mine. Hard, desperate, hungry.

I leaned into the kiss, talking with my body, pouring every second of stress and worry and guilt into the spots where our lips touched. I needed him to know how I felt about him, how much I cared for him, and words weren't working anymore.

But when we finished kissing, the glazed look had returned to his eyes. He stood up and straightened out his clothes, and I did the same.

"Ready to go?" he asked.

No. But I just said, "Let's go."

Cars lined the streets so tightly around the party that traffic could only go in one direction. We drove around for nearly an hour looking for a parking spot and only managed to find one because someone was leaving. It took me fifteen minutes to parallel park in the spot barely big enough for a Vespa, and we were still three blocks away.

By the third time Jon nearly got knocked over on the sidewalk, I was over the night and ready to go home.

I glanced over at him, at his even expression that

hid everything going on under the surface. I wanted to tell him about Stormy and Braxton Hicks and labor and all the emotions swirling inside, but I couldn't. They wouldn't reach him anyway with his mind a million miles from me.

When we finally got to the house, there were drunk people hanging on the porch. One of them made a comment about Jon being a cripple.

I sent him a glare that could singe ash.

We walked into the crowded house, and someone immediately called out to Jon. "Hey, man, we're playing pong in the garage! Come out!"

Jon nodded. "For sure."

"You wanna drink?" the guy asked.

"Yeah," Jon answered. "A beer?"

I did a double take. Was I even here with the right guy? As his friend went off to get Jon a beer, I asked. "What are you doing?"

"I'm getting a drink."

"Why?"

He looked over his shoulder, toward the other party goers. "It's not like I have to worry about getting kicked off the track team anymore."

I stared at him, at a loss. "You've never even drunk anything before."

"Guess it's time to start," Jon said like my words didn't matter at all.

His friend came back with a beer, then seeming to realize Jon was on crutches, said, "Follow me. You can have it when we get out to the garage."

We followed the guy down a few cement stairs to a garage that was only slightly less crowded. But when you factored in the lawn-care equipment and giant kennel with a pit bull inside, it felt just as bad.

"Look who came!" the guy called to the others.

"Finally!" another one yelled. "I call him for my team."

Another friend looked me over. "Then I get her."

Jon said, "She's mine. But you can borrow her."

Who even was my boyfriend? I'd never heard him say anything like that before. He definitely didn't talk about me like I wasn't there. Like I was a possession to be passed around.

His friend, who looked like a taller, beefier version of Frank, walked over to me. "You any good?"

"No," I deadpanned. I didn't want to be here, much less be buddy-buddy and drink with a stranger who was "borrowing" me for a game. Jon and I'd have a lot to talk about when we got home.

But for now, I was getting handed sticky ping-pong balls and being told to throw it at a cup or else I'd have to drink.

When I missed the first throw, the guy handed me a beer, but I shook my head. "I drove."

"Come on, one won't kill you."

"I drove," I repeated.

"Give her a pop," Jon said dismissively like he was tired of the argument.

With a groan, the guy disappeared into the kitchen and came back with a root beer. I didn't want to add any sugary calories, but I wasn't about to belabor the point. I just wanted this night to be over.

My partner and I won three out of five, and he tried to rope me into a second round, but I refused.

"That's okay," Jon slurred. "She can sit by me over here."

He dropped onto the dog crate and patted the spot beside him. Thank god the dog was way less vicious than it looked.

I just shook my head and folded my arms over my chest before going to Jon and whispering, "What are we doing here, Jon?"

He drained the rest of his drink. "Partying, Abi. Having *fun*. For once in my life."

I couldn't help the hurt that sparked in my chest at his words. "We've never had fun?"

"I didn't mean it like that."

He reached out for my arm, and I begrudgingly let him hold my hand.

"Aw, Abi," he said. "I didn't mean to hurt your feelings. I love you. Like more than anything. You're seriously the best girl in the world. Check out the girls in this room? You're the best. In the state? You're the best. In the world? No contest."

I rolled my eyes, stifling a smile. "Well, I think you're pretty great too." Most of the time. "And drunk."

He wrapped his arms around my waist and hugged my stomach. "I love you so much."

I patted his head while making a mental checklist to get him a cold shower and a long night's sleep. "I love you too."

"Let's get out of here?"

"Thought you'd never ask."

CHAPTER FORTY-ONE

WHEN WE GOT out the front door and back into the cold air, I asked, "Where do you want to go?"

He shrugged. "I think there's a park nearby."

"We can drive there?"

"No, let's walk."

I wasn't going to argue with him. Maybe walking it off in the chilly weather would do him good. I tucked my hands deeper into my coat pockets and walked alongside him, quiet. Thinking.

"Drinking is weird," Jon said.

I snorted. "Seeing you drinking is weird."

"I've missed out on so much trying to be a track star," Jon said.

My heart went out to him. "You would have won

nationals, and you're only a freshman. You *were* a track star, Jon."

"Exactly. Past tense." His jaw tightened, and his lips formed a heavy, regretful line. "And for what?"

"A chance," I said. "No one promised you it would work out the way you wanted or planned. If it wasn't a ski pole, it could have been a car hitting you in the road, a pothole on the corn run, a—"

"I don't want to talk about it."

The coldness in his words made me recoil, but then he softened and added, "I want to talk about the good things in my life." He nodded toward the park coming into view ahead of us. "The fact that there are two adult swings up there." He glanced up. "And I can see the moon. You."

A corner of my lips lifted. "I see where I rank."

He laughed. "It wasn't listed in order of importance."

"I can't believe you can say importance four beers deep."

A smile crossed his face. The first one in a while. "I'm feeling better. Just a little...fuzzy."

"You're buzzing."

"Mhmm." He dropped his crutches on the wood chips and settled into one of the swings. "It feels nice. Maybe I should drink more often."

I sat in the open swing and toed the ground. I wanted to tell him no, he should never pick up a beer again, but who was I to say that? How could I explain that he needed to see drinking as casual, not as a means of escape? I'd seen first-hand where using substances for relief could lead. Lived under the same roof as two abusers and promised myself I would never live with one again.

"You think too much," Jon said.

I leaned on the swing chain and looked over at him. "What do you mean?"

"We're young, free; we should be having fun."

"Okay, Wiz Khalifa," I drawled.

He chuckled. "You're funny too."

"One of my many likable qualities."

"You do have quite a few."

"Mm?"

"Yeah," he said. "You're cute as hell. So damn sexy—"

"Okay, now I know you're still drunk."

"Psh." He reached out and drew my swing closer so my knees were touching his brace. His eyes traveled my body and held my gaze. "My favorite thing about you, though? You fight for what you want, and you make it happen."

If that was true, why did my heart feel like it was

breaking right now? Like I was on a treadmill going just a little too fast, ready to fling me off the second I slowed down?

Still, I managed a smile. "Thank you."

"You know," he said. "You're kind of perfect."

"Now you're just being over the top."

He shook his head. "I'm serious, Abi."

"Oh." What else could I say?

"In all the things I'd imagined in a future wife...you're it. And the fact that you've stayed with me through this." He gestured at his leg. "I know you'll always be here for me."

"Of course, Jon." I reached out and took his hand, trying not to show the fact that I was shaking about his use of the w-word. "I never expected life to be easy. Just better with you by my side."

He stood up from the swing, practically dragging me to my feet. "Marry me, Abi?"

My mouth hung open. Only one word came out even though a million went through my mind. "What?"

His eyes were wide as he struggled to stay standing in front of me, swaying on one leg. "I'm serious. I love you. You love me. What are we waiting for?"

The thudding of blood rushed through my ears as Jon's words crashed into my mind.

He just asked me to marry him. But it felt wrong. There was still beer on his breath.

"Jon, let's go home," I said.

"Why?" he asked, a troubled look crossing his expression as he wobbled.

"You're drunk," I said. "I'll go get the car."

"But…" He sat back on the swing, making the chains rattle. "You're not going to say yes?"

Now the tears were coming—for both of us. "Of course I'm not going to say yes!" I cried.

He barely met my eyes. "You don't want to marry me."

More than anything. I wanted to marry Jon Scoller more than anything. But this guy sitting in front of me, I didn't know who he was. "Not like this," I said, wiping at tears. "Do you even a have a plan now?"

"What do you mean, 'a plan'?"

"For your future!" I cried. "What do you want to do? What are you going to do without track?"

"*You* are my future, Abi. Nothing else matters."

My lips trembled. "You're a mess, Jon."

Temper leached into his voice. "How could you say that?"

"Because, it's the truth," I said. And then it hit me. "You're just like my dad. He had an injury and let it control his life. Let drugs and emotions rule instead of his mind. And now I'm with a guy who'd just proposed to me sitting on a park swing, three sheets to the wind."

"How could you say that?" he demanded.

"Because it's true," I said, dropping into the swing myself. "This wasn't supposed to be how it went," I cried. "You were supposed to get your act together, figure out that you had more than running. That you had me. How can you know you want to marry me when you don't even know who you are?"

Jon's mouth opened and closed, but finally an angry expression covered his face. "You should leave me if I'm such a burden."

"That's not what I'm saying—"

"You should go," he said. "You have better things to do." He stood up and got his crutches. "I'm getting a cab. Don't follow me."

I stared at the man I used to love as his transformation to a stranger became complete. And then I walked the opposite direction.

CHAPTER FORTY-TWO

I COULDN'T BRING myself to go back to the place where we'd spent so many moments together. Where he'd given me a taste of forever with the real him before offering it with this new stranger.

Instead, I went to a coffee shop that stayed open late so people could study and ordered a smoothie. The fruit tasted like chalk though. My throat didn't want to let anything into my churning stomach.

Maybe because I'd let my everything just walk away.

From the look on his face, an apology wouldn't make this up. I'd broken his heart just as surely as he'd broken mine. And now, what were we? It felt like we were two pieces of ice that had broken apart and were now drifting aimlessly, seconds from melting and being lost altogether.

One of the employees approached me and said the shop was closing.

I just nodded and dumped my smoothie in the trash on the way out. I needed to go home—to the dorm. My new home.

Deep down, I hoped Jon would be waiting for me in the hallway when I got there, saying he was sorry, that he was joking, that he had a plan and a ring and that he'd thought through the proposal just as thoroughly as I'd daydreamed of forever with him.

But when I reached the hallway to my room, it was completely empty. With my heart weighing heavily, I trudged to my room, unlocked the door, and walked inside. Alone.

Part of me wanted to drive straight to Woodman and curl up next to Grandma on the couch while she comforted me, but I knew I needed sleep after everything that had happened. So, I crawled into my bed and curled under the covers, lying still until crying led to exhaustion and finally sleep.

Pounding on the door woke me hours later. I had no idea how long I'd slept, but the light outside was stronger than the wan morning rays I'd come to expect.

I rubbed my puffy eyes and stumbled toward the door.

There was Jon on the other side.

My muscles failed me, freezing in place. But not as much as my brain had let me down. Why hadn't I planned something to say? Something to do? I didn't want to lose Jon, even if I didn't want to marry him right now.

"Abi," he said. But that was all. Just my name.

I leaned my forehead against the doorframe, giving him a weary stare. "Yeah?"

He looked tortured, from his crumpled shirt to the circles under his eyes. He had slept in the same clothes he'd worn the night before. "I need you," he said. "And I think that's why I have to let you go."

My heart plummeted, sank, hard as a rock into my stomach, where pure panic took over. "You don't need to leave me."

"I do." He clutched at his own chest. "I can't take it. You're the only thing I look forward to every day, Abi. You're keeping me going."

"Jon, don't do this," I cried, coming to my senses. He was breaking up with me. My mind couldn't make sense of it—couldn't comprehend the ripping sensation in my chest.

"You're all I have left, Abi." He spread his arms

wide. "There's nothing left of me. My identity can't be *you*."

"That's not true," I argued, even though I knew he'd never see how untrue that statement was while he was in this state.

Jon simply shook his head.

"You just need to see that you're more than your running." Desperation filled my voice. "You *are*."

His eyes softened. "After everything you've been through, Abi, you deserve better than"—his voice cracked, and he swallowed—"better than me."

"Jon, that's not true," I said forcefully. "You're amazing."

"If I were, we wouldn't be standing here, saying this," he argued. "We'd be calling our families to tell them we're engaged."

"No." I shook my head. "You just...Give me more time, Jon. Maybe I was just scared."

"I didn't even have a ring." He lifted my hand with the promise ring. "This means more than anything I said last night."

I clenched my jaw. "So what, we're throwing it all away because you said something stupid the first time you drank?"

"It's more than that." He kissed my hand, the ring. "If I have any chance at becoming the kind of man you deserve, I need some time. I need to focus on me, whoever that is."

My throat tightened, and I tried, failed, to swallow space for me to talk without crying. "But what about what I want?" Tears streamed over my cheeks. "I can't lose you."

He wiped at his own tears. "You already have." He turned to leave, his crutches crackling on the tile.

"Jon!" I called after him, but he didn't stop. "Jon, please. Come back."

But he ignored me, and once again, the love of my life was walking away. The truth I didn't want to admit swelled in my chest and flooded out my eyes: he'd already been gone a while now.

CHAPTER FORTY-THREE

I'D GONE into survival mode after that, numb to everything, even the icy air that fogged every breath I took.

Now, on my way to my last class of the day, I just wanted it to be over so I could sleep away the pain I knew was waiting for me.

My phone rang, interrupting the music playing through my earbuds. Anika's name lit up my screen, and I slid it over to answer. We'd missed each other this morning, but she hardly ever called me.

"Hello?" I said, concerned.

"What's going on with Jon?" she asked.

"What do you mean?" Just hearing his name made my knees weak and shaky. I stepped off the sidewalk to avoid getting ran over by everyone else during the class change.

"Kyle said he's moving to a new dorm but wouldn't say why."

All the breath I had escaped my chest, and I couldn't get any back in. I clutched a light pole, desperately trying to stay upright. "He's moving?"

"You didn't know?" Concern laced her voice. "What's going on?"

"Jon, he—" I clenched my teeth against the wail trying to escape. "He proposed."

"He what?!" she cried. "Am I missing something? Are you two moving out?"

The idea of a future where Jon and I could move in together, get our own place, just seemed cruel now. "No, I said no. And he...left me."

"Abi," she gasped. "What—you said—where are you? Are you okay?"

"I'm on my way to poli sci." I swallowed down acid. "And I'm not okay."

"Skip it," she said.

"I can't miss class. I—"

"You're not going to learn anything anyway," she insisted. "You're obviously too ups—"

"I need to go. I can't think about this." A tear

slipped out my eye and chilled on my cheek. I swiped it away. "I'll see you tonight?"

"I'll be here. With ice cream," she promised.

I hung up and let go of the light pole. The only way to keep from collapsing was to keep moving. Just like Jon was.

Halfway through my class, my phone began chiming quietly in my pocket. Since I'd sat in the back, the prof couldn't hear it. Still, I switched it to silent mode and watched as the messages came through in an old group text. One without Jon or Michele in it.

Stormy: Facebook says Jon's single.

Stormy: What happened?

Evan: What???

Skye: Are you okay?

Macy: Does it have to do with his injury?

Skye: We're here for you, girl, when you're ready to talk.

Roberto: I'll kill him for you.

Andrew: I've got the shovel.

Andrew: And some time before the wedding.

Evan: I'm in. My trunk's pretty big.

Roberto: Let's meet at 0300. I think I can get to some weapons...

Despite myself, I managed a smile. But it didn't last. Jon was still gone. I was still single. I typed out the truth.

Abi: Jon left me. I'm not ready to talk about it.

No one replied. I could only imagine the texts going through their phones, without me.

The lack of messages didn't last, though, because Nikki had seen the post too.

Nikki: What happened? Are you okay? Why didn't you say anything this morning?

I sighed to myself. Anika was right. I wasn't learning anything today.

I sent a new text to Anika and Nikki.

Abi: Meet me in the dorm.

Abi: And bring the ice cream.

When I made it back to my room, Anika was already there, and Nikki arrived within five minutes carrying three separate pints. Wordlessly, I picked the most chocolatey one there was and peeled back the top.

She handed me a spoon, and I shoveled a bite into my mouth, letting the flavor hit as tears oozed out of me.

How was this me? How was this Jon?

"We were supposed to make it," I sobbed. "We were supposed to be forever."

But forever hadn't lasted nearly as long as I'd thought it would.

CHAPTER FORTY-FOUR

THE NEXT WEEK passed like a kidney stone.

Each day, I hoped it would get better, that my heart would stop feeling like it was being rolled around in shards of glass, but deep down, I knew there wasn't an easy fix to this.

I'd given myself to Jon in every way a person could, and now, I couldn't get it back. No matter how much Stormy cursed his very existence or how many inspirational notes Anika left on my desk or how often Nikki told me to pour my pain into track, I couldn't make it better.

So far, time wasn't working either. Not seven days. Not fourteen. Not even a month made the constant ache in my chest subside.

Cue my college friends' hare-brained idea.

Nikki, Mollie, and Jayne barged into our room—
with Anika holding the door wide open—and began
a makeover, making my transformation complete
with makeup, hair, and a ridiculous outfit.

They had me done up and dressed down in less
than twenty minutes.

"I'm going to freeze to death," I argued, looking
at the short skirt and midriff sweater in the mirror.
At least they'd had the decency to give me some
sleeves.

"We'll be inside all night," Nikki reminded me.
"It's always hot in the bars."

Jayne gave me a concerned look, then spoke to
Nikki. "Are you sure she's ready?"

Nikki looked me straight on. "If you don't want
to go, if you think going out will make things worse,
just say the word. But don't stay home, in your dorm,
because of Jon. Stay for you."

I swallowed thickly and looked at the stranger in
the mirror. I would do anything to make the pain in
her eyes go away.

"Exactly," Nikki said.

Anika gripped my hand. "Come on. You look
amazing."

"You look comfortable," I quipped. I wished I
could trade my outfit for her jeans and boots.

She shook her head and whispered, "I'm the only one who looks comfortable."

I managed a smile. That was the truth.

Nikki walked to the door. "I'll pick you up in front of the building. So you don't freeze."

I gave her a two-finger salute. One finger with these press-on nails probably would have done the job.

While Jayne and Mollie went with her, Anika and I took our time walking down to the lobby. We didn't have to worry about running into Jon anymore since he'd move to an entirely different dorm. Apparently, I'd taken custody of this building without even asking for it.

We got into Mollie's car and squeezed into the backseat. A glittery flask got passed around, and I took a few sips, even though my heart wasn't in it. Was this what getting over someone looked like? Felt like?

I didn't have time to think about it, because we reached Freddie Mash and the other girls practically shoved us out the backseat. Anika and I paid our way in while they went to park. There were a lot of people inside, so many we had to squeeze our way around the edges of the dance floor to find an open spot to stand.

I took in all the people dancing, laughing, drinking, and tried to keep my eyes off of all the couples who looked absolutely, painfully, in love. They were everywhere—swaying close on the dance floor, standing against walls with their lips pressed together, ordering drinks at the bar, laughing, talking.

I focused on Anika and yelled over the music, "Is Kyle coming out?"

She shook her head and offered me a smile. "I figured it would be a girls' night."

I gripped her hand as a thank you.

"So, what do you want to do?" she asked.

I shrugged. I wasn't much of a dancer. Plus, I couldn't drink until the girls brought in their hand sanitizer to scrub off the under-age mark—if I even wanted to.

"Crowd-surfing?" she asked with a wink.

A smile started before the pain hit my chest. I'd done it for Jon, to see him happy. The memory felt like one of the many parts of me that belonged to him now.

"Abi!" Nikki yelled, a tall guy with dark hair and even darker eyes walking behind her. "Have you met my friend Josh?"

I tried to smile at him as I shook my head. He

was tall, dark, and handsome in every sense of the words, but it did nothing for me.

He held out his hand, and it enveloped mine, large and warm and rough. He held on a little longer than he needed to as he leaned in and drawled, "Nice to meet you, Abi."

A dormant part of me twitched, not quite ready to come to life. "You too."

Still holding my hand, he asked, "Want to dance?"

Nikki answered for me. "Of course she does."

He led me through the couples to the dance floor and easily swept me into his chest, leading us in a slow two-step I somehow managed to follow. Josh held me close, but not too close. His hand on my waist was firm, but not suggestive. Under his cowboy hat, his eyes stayed on my face, on the other dancers. He was being a perfect gentleman, and all I could think about was Jon and the sock hop and how he'd told me I was one of a kind.

"Do you go to school here?" Josh asked.

"Upton," I said. "You?"

"The tech school," he replied. "Carpentry."

That explained his hands. "How do you know Nikki?"

"We grew up together."

I nodded. He wasn't just some rebound guy then. She was trying to set me up for a real relationship.

I didn't know how I felt about that, but he didn't give me time to figure it out. As the song sped up, he spun me in an easy turn.

My eyes widened as he drew me back to his chest and started a faster two-step. "I can't dance!"

He laughed. "Looks like you're doing alright to me."

We worked through two songs before I had to take a break. "I'm tired! You keep dancing."

"No way." He shook his head. "I owe you a drink."

He got me a Coke at the bar, then poured something from a flask inside when no one was looking.

"Whiskey," he explained.

I didn't want to drink it—my parents always drank whiskey and vodka—but I managed a sip.

"You hate it," he said.

"I hate it," I admitted.

Laughing, he took it away and left it on the bar. A slow song came over the speakers, and his eyes lit up. "I love this one."

The light in his expression warmed me, and I

wanted more of that feeling. I'd do anything for it. "Let's dance."

Again, he led me to the dance floor, but instead of a fast-paced swing, he held me closer than before and swayed along to the music, singing to each word of this country song about heartbreak and starting over new.

The words hit me right in the chest.

I broke down, right there in the middle of the dance floor, and sobbed into Josh's chest knowing no amount of music or ice cream or chocolatey brown eyes would ever—*ever*—make getting over Jon any easier. My heart was his.

CHAPTER FORTY-FIVE

I FINISHED PACKING clothes for the next few days while Anika sat on the edge of her bed.

"Are you sure you're going to be okay?" she asked. "Won't it be hard, going home?"

I shrugged in answer to both of her questions, keeping my eyes down. "He'll still be in class the first few days I'm back for the hearing, and then I can come and stay in the dorms over spring break, so I won't have to see him."

We both knew that didn't matter. Even if Jon stayed in Austin, his memories still lived in Woodman. I'd drive right past the spot where I met him on the bus the first time. I'd walk up the steps where he'd come to pick me up for school each morning. I'd fall asleep in the bed where I'd had my first time with him and then woken up in his arms.

"Do his parents know you broke up?" Anika asked. "Aren't they close with your grandma?"

I turned my back to her and shrugged. This new subject wasn't much better than the last one. Plus, it reminded me I needed to tell my grandma what had happened. How, I didn't know.

"Sorry," she said. "I just...I can't imagine how I'd handle it if Kyle and I broke up."

I busied my fingers and my mind with going over my mental checklist. There was nothing left to do here. And if I forgot something, Grandma would have extra or help me find some.

"I guess I better get on the road," I said.

Anika slid down from her bunk and then came to give me a hug. She held on long enough to make my eyes water. Why did hugs always make me want to fall apart?

She patted my back. "Call me, text me, if you need anything. Okay?" She pulled back and added, "I mean it."

I nodded, blinking quickly. "I will."

She held the door open for me, and I walked down the hall toward the elevators, rolling my bag behind me. Deep down, I wished I would run into

Jon. I hadn't seen him, heard from him, or seen any new posts on social media since we split up over a month ago.

It was the longest we'd gone without talking since we'd met. I missed him like I'd miss my right arm if it suddenly disappeared. No matter how much I tried to shove thoughts of him to a back corner of my mind, they always surfaced.

There was no sign of him on the way to my car. With disappointment spreading in my chest, I threw my bag in the trunk, got in, and started down the road. For two hours, I fought the memories, playing the music so loud I couldn't hear myself think.

Grandma's house had never been such a welcome sight. Not when I was a little kid coming for a visit. Not when I first moved in with three garbage bags of my stuff. Not even when I first came home from college.

Now, I pulled into the drive and ran to the front door, barely stifling tears that had been falling the entire trip home. I let myself inside and looked for her.

I found her curled up on the couch under an electric blanket, watching a movie.

"Abi? You're home early." At the look on my face, she said, "What's wrong, honey?"

Instead of answering, I got on the couch and lay with my head in her lap, crying as she brushed my hair back and soothed me.

"I thought I could do it," I sobbed. "I thought I could help him, but it's all wrong. He doesn't want my help. He's not even himself anymore."

She softly shushed me. "Slow down, honey. I'm sure it will be okay."

"He broke up with me, Grandma. It's over between us."

A quiet gasp escaped her chest. "Did he say why?"

"He said I deserve better and that he needs time to work on himself. Why couldn't he do that while we were together?" A sob made me cough. "My parents don't even love me. I don't know why I expected him to."

Her voice was firm. "Nothing you did or didn't do could have changed this. Don't you dare take responsibility for any of it."

A million arguments came to mind. I was too demanding, too much trouble, too much drama, too much of everything bad and not enough of anything good. "But—"

"No," she snapped, then forced me to look her in the eyes. "They are their own responsibility. You never should have had to take care of your parents or hide their secrets. Jon chose to go snowboarding that day, and a freak accident happened. *He* decided to stay down instead of get back up. It is not your fault. *You* are your responsibility. You take care of that first."

I wiped at my eyes. "But what if I lost him forever?"

She shook her head. "Guys like Jon never stay down for long. Especially when they have a woman who demands they rise to the occasion."

CHAPTER FORTY-SIX

STORMY CAME over that evening after work. She looked way bigger than the last time I'd seen her, but I was smart enough not to say so.

Grandma, on the other hand, walked right over and rubbed Stormy's belly. "You're getting so big!"

Stormy didn't seem to mind. She covered one of Grandma's hands with her own and moved it. "Can you feel her kicking?"

My eyes widened. "Her?"

Her smile spread. "Her."

"How exciting!" Grandma clapped.

And it was exciting. But it was also hard to understand how so much happiness and loss could exist in the same room. It made me want to walk away so I wouldn't bring down the mood.

But that was the old Abi thinking. My therapist had said that removing myself from hard circumstances and people I love was a coping mechanism—an unhealthy one. I breathed through my feelings and then went to give Stormy a hug. I told her I was happy for her, because I was.

We stood in silence for a few minutes, the three of us, and then Stormy turned to Grandma and said, "Is it okay if I steal your girl?"

"Go right on ahead," Grandma said. "Just make sure she's back in the morning." And then she met my eyes. "If she wants to be."

Grandma was giving me an out to miss the parole hearing, but I'd meant what I'd said that morning in the living room with Jon and his parents when they suggested I quit. I didn't want to have any part in letting my dad walk free. And Grandma was right; I deserved to have the last word.

Stormy had me come out to her car with her, and we started down the road.

"What's the plan?" I asked.

She gave me a smile. "How does a good distraction sound?"

"Like Dorian Gray singing a love song personally written for me."

That drew a laugh. "Well, then. Get ready for the best love song of your life."

Her car turned toward the highway going out of town. "Where are we going?" I asked. "Are you kidnapping me?"

"Kind of?" She said it like a question, which just made me laugh.

"How can you 'kind of' kidnap someone?" And then I realized I was laughing about being kidnapped when a few months ago I would have been having flashbacks.

Instead of making me upset, it made me proud. I'd managed a joke, a normal conversation, without breaking down in a panic.

"I think it's okay to take you since your Grandma said so."

"So, no clues?"

She shrugged. "I thought we could do something a little different."

A sign saying we had twenty miles left until we reached Roderdale flashed outside my window.

"We're not going to Roderdale, are we?"

"Dammit," she swore under her breath. "I knew I should have made you wear Frank's blindfold."

My cheeks heated. "I don't need to know anything more about Frank's blindfold."

"Get your mind out of the gutter. He wears it to sleep!"

"Most people call that an eye mask," I argued. "Plus...you're kind of pregnant."

"Kind of?" she mocked me. "How can someone be 'kind of' pregnant?"

"You can be 'kind of' a jerk too," I said pointedly.

"Whatever, you love me." She laughed and cranked the radio to her normal-Stormy volume. Too loud to talk, almost too loud to think, and she sang along to her playlist.

Eventually, she turned off the highway into Roderdale and drove to the school. I'd never been there before, but it looked about like McClellan and Woodman—all red brick and flat roofs—just smaller.

Once the car was off, and the deafening music with it, I asked, "What are we doing here?"

"I don't think we ever went to a basketball game in high school. At least, not together. It could be fun to go. Be really obnoxious. Cheer like we know someone there." She unclasped her seatbelt. "If we're feeling really rowdy, I can pretend I'm going into labor."

I rolled my eyes and got out of the car. "You're crazy."

She looked at me over the hood. "Is that code for the next YouTube prank sensation?"

"Not exactly."

"Plus, I love me some nacho cheese." She swung her purse over her shoulder and started toward the door. "Do you think they'd put it on a pickle for me?"

"Ew, seriously?"

After sending a hurt stare my way, she rubbed her belly and spoke to it. "Don't worry. Auntie Abi didn't mean to hurt your feelings."

"Uh huh." I pushed the school door open and held it for her. "Blame the baby."

"What other benefits are there to being pregnant?" she asked. "I mean, other than the whole hair and nails thing?"

"Maybe the precious new life thing?" I teased.

She tilted her head. "Good point."

We walked down an empty hallway, following signs to the gym. Somewhere in the distance, I could hear whistles and the occasional cheer. "Why aren't there more people here?" I asked.

"I mean, it is Roderdale," she said. "There's no one here. Wanna break into some unlocked cars later?"

I pretended to consider it. "Rain check?"

"Right, that might be too much excitement."

"We don't want you going into labor." I laughed.

After a few turns past trophy cases that still displayed plaques from the '50s, we made it to the cafeteria next to the gym. She paid the five bucks for us to get in and then spent twenty at the concession stand.

As she checked out, I muttered, "Are you Octomom or something?"

She rolled her eyes. "I'll let you have some too, don't worry."

"That's not really what I was worried about..."

She was already walking into the gym with her tower of food, though, scouting chairs. Plus, this was the girl who had no shame. Making her first impression in a strange place balancing three plates filled with cheese-covered items was the least of her concerns.

She led me up to a spot near the back of the gym where we could sit on the bleachers with our backs against the wall. High school guys played on the court, and the scoreboard said they were still in the first quarter.

With cheese on her top lip, Stormy yelled, "GO, TEAM! YOU GOT THIS!"

A few people around us turned to stare. Probably because nothing was really happening in the game.

Not that I'd actually know what an exciting moment was. This was my first basketball game, that I remembered at least.

"You have to try this," she said and handed me a plate with popcorn and a puddle of barbecue sauce.

"Seriously?"

She nodded enthusiastically. "Better than a personalized Dorian Gray song."

"Like anything could top that."

Refusing to take no for an answer, she dipped a kernel herself and handed it to me. Salty barbecue flavor inundated my taste buds, blending with the buttery popcorn. It was all I could do to keep from moaning.

I leaned over her stomach. "Baby girl, I take it back. You have amazing taste."

Stormy laughed, making her stomach wobble.

A guy wearing the visiting team's jersey made a basket, and Stormy let out a loud whoop.

"I don't think that's the right team," I muttered.

She shrugged, so I started cheering with her.

If you can't beat 'em, join 'em, right?

CHAPTER FORTY-SEVEN

AS PROMISED, Stormy brought me to Grandma's house after the game, and I went straight to my room. Without the distraction of the buzzers and players and Stormy's too-loud music, my thoughts ran wild.

Just like I'd expected, memories of Jon fought for attention, striking me one after another. Not just from our relationship, but from all the time I'd known him. The thrill of him picking me up. The shock of seeing him and Denise together in the kitchen. The butterflies that shot through me the first time he'd said he loved me.

I stared at my bed, wondering if I should just sleep on the floor, but then I remembered Jon coming in before my first day of work with his dad, my period-stained underwear laundry on full display.

The only thing that could come close to tearing my thoughts away was the next day's task. I pulled my comforter and pillows to the floor and lay down with the speech I'd prepared. I whispered it out loud, trying to picture how I could make it better—deliver it so the board had no choice but to make him serve his full term.

Eventually, my eyes became dry and the letters began blurring. I physically couldn't stay awake anymore. So, I set the paper beside me and fell asleep right there on my bedroom floor.

Grandma woke me in the morning, a sad, knowing look on her face. "You okay, sweetie?"

I gave a jerky shake of my head as I stretched out the knots in my back. No use lying.

She extended her hand to help me up, and I took it, not putting any weight on her grip.

"What time is it?" I asked.

"Eight. We have about an hour and a half before we need to leave."

"Right." I nodded. "Right."

I used the chore of getting ready to take my mind off the day and the churning in my stomach. I wanted Dad to see how good I looked now that I was no longer under his thumb. I wanted him to see that I was happy and healthy—even if one of those was a stretch right now. But I would be happy again. I hoped.

After putting on a pair of slacks and a plain dress shirt I used to wear to work with Mr. Scoller, I slipped on some black flats and went to the living room where Grandma waited, looking impeccable.

When she noticed me, she stood and grabbed her purse. "Ready?"

"No," I said. "But yes."

With a nod, she started toward the door. "We're walking to the Scollers' house, and then we'll ride with Glen and Marta."

"Marta's coming too?"

"Yes," she said as she locked the deadbolt. "She wants to be there for you."

"Does she know...about..."

I let my sentence hang, waiting for Grandma to fill in the blanks.

She kept her gaze ahead and nodded.

But that just left more questions. Had Jon told them? Did Grandma let them know last night? And if the Scollers had known, had they kept it secret from Grandma? Was she surprised when I told her last night? Were they mad at me? Or worse, disappointed?

I worried the questions would follow me all the

way to the prison, but then Glen came out the front door and wrapped me in the most fatherly hug I'd experienced in my entire life.

He held me tight as he said, "We're here for you, Abi, no matter what."

Tears found my eyes, and I struggled to swallow the lump in my throat. "Thank you" was all I could manage, although it didn't even come close to being enough.

Marta put her arms around us, too, completing a classic Scoller group hug. Just the thought made my chest hurt more, knowing it would never be complete again. Deep down, I'd been looking forward to having them as in-laws someday. As second parents. Now, that was just a fantasy. A dream from another life.

The only thing that could have snapped me out of the self-pitying pain in my chest was the sight of Jon's white car, coming down the road, parking in front of his parents' house.

Every muscle in my body rendered itself ineffective. I'd wanted him to text me, to call me, to come to my dorm and tell me it had all been a mistake. But here he was, walking toward us, a smaller brace on his leg, crutches-free. His hair had grown out, covered his forehead in a messy fringe. He looked...different. But the same. This was Jon, but he wasn't mine anymore.

As if realizing I was standing with his parents, he froze. "What—what're you doing here?"

Somehow my voice came out clear, cool, foreign. "My dad's parole hearing is today."

He looked between me and his dad, anger suddenly reworking his features. "You didn't tell me?"

"I—" I began, but Glen stepped in.

"You had no right to know anymore." Then he added, "And you weren't supposed to be home until this evening."

"Classes got cancelled, and I—that's not the point." He looked directly at me. "Of course I want to be there for you, Abi. I promised I would be there for you. Why wouldn't you tell me?"

My mouth opened and closed, shocked at the indignation in his voice. He'd promised a lot of things, none of which he intended to keep. At least, not anymore.

Glen reached up and clamped a hand on his son's shoulder. "You follow me." He marched Jon toward the door, but not fast enough for me to miss him saying, "You do not need to cause that girl any more pain than you already have."

CHAPTER FORTY-EIGHT

MARTA WOULDN'T MEET my eyes before getting in the car, but I didn't miss her sniffing.

Grandma rubbed my back, walking me toward the door to the back seat. "Ready to go, sweetheart?"

I nodded and breathed, "As ready as I'll ever be."

She sat in the back with me, and when Glen returned, he twisted in the seat and said, "Abi, I'm sorry for that. Is there anything I can do?"

Erase the past, I wanted to say.

Instead, I settled for a small shake of my head and the ghost of a smile.

He put the vehicle in reverse, and before long, their house and the sight of Jon was a painful memory battling with my fear for the challenge I was about to face.

After two hours of driving, the men's correctional faculty came into view before us, all brick walls and chain-link fence and spiraling barbed wire.

"Ready?" Glen asked, looking directly at me in the rear-view mirror.

Unable to speak, I nodded.

Glen said the parole hearing would be in a smaller trial room, with a board that discussed my father's behavior in prison. The board members would decide whether he got to leave. And I should prepare myself for either outcome.

As if that were possible.

We opened the car doors and spilled out of the vehicle. Began walking in a mismatched, informal formation toward the prison.

After searching us all, the CO led us to a room with old red chairs and wood-paneled walls. When he closed the door behind us, it felt like he was closing us in, trapping us.

Grandma sat beside me, held my hand. She was here for me, always. I knew it. Felt it.

My other hand shook on the paper I held. The speech I'd prepared for this day in the limited time I had. Even if I'd had years to write and revise and envision this moment in my head, I never would have been prepared to see them walking my father into the room, handcuffed in an orange jumpsuit. His hair was grayer than it had been a year ago. His eyes harder, with deeper wrinkles at the corners.

I wanted him to look at me, to see the person I'd become, no thanks to him. To see the people I had surrounding me, even when he'd failed his basic job as a father to love and protect me. But he kept his eyes straight ahead, ignoring me completely.

They started the hearing talking about why he was in prison. What he had done. The brief synopsis did nothing to encompass the years of suffering I'd experienced at his meaty, unforgiving hands. And then they spoke about his behavior in prison. Said he kept to himself. That he was well-behaved, polite even, to guards and the warden.

Bile rose in my throat. Of course he was on his best behavior here. Dad had always been great at pretending like he wasn't a walking piece of shit.

My hand clenched on Grandma's. How could they be saying such positive words about someone who had left so much wreckage in his wake?

She squeezed back, sharing some of her strength with me.

Someone spoke my name. Glen.

"It's your turn," he said.

They told me to approach the microphone. To

say my piece. My hands shook on the paper so much I had to take a deep breath and steady myself before I could read the words.

"The last thing this man said to me, the man you're here to make a decision about, was that I would pay for what I'd done to him. He's lived in these prison walls for a year and a half now, and I can tell you he's nowhere close to paying for everything he's done."

I shared the story of how he was injured. How his mood spiraled out of control when he had to stay home after the surgery and couldn't work. How he used to beat me on his benders and how a good night was when I found him passed out on the couch, usually next to a half-empty bottle of whiskey or vodka.

I shared how pills suddenly lined our medicine cabinet and would come and go as Dad made his mysterious trips and came back after days away. I now knew he was going to South Texas, getting drugs from people across the border.

And then I looked right at him, into his dishwater-blue eyes, which were so much like my own, as I said, "Do not be fooled by the act he puts on when in front of people more powerful than him. This man deserves every second of the sentence he was handed, and letting him out in the world would be a danger to everyone around him, especially those who are weaker." I stared at him harder, willing him to feel every single word as much as I did. "As his daughter who lived under his roof for eighteen torturous years, I know exactly the kind of man he is, and he is not the kind who deserves to walk free."

His eyes flared with the anger I knew lived inside him every day, and his lips formed a tight line that used to always precede a beating. He knew I'd meant every single one of my words. I just hoped the parole board had *heard* them.

The parole board left the hearing room. I tried to tell from their expressions whether or not my speech had meant anything to them, but they were blank slates, hiding all emotion. A CO walked Dad out of the room in handcuffs, back to his cell.

We could only wait.

After what felt like hours, the board returned to the wooden room, a CO bringing my father in again with him. My heart raced as they returned to their seats, and the person in the middle of the board cleared his throat.

"We have determined Mr. Johnson is not to receive parole at this time. He will continue serving his sentence as ruled by the..."

But I didn't hear the rest of the words. I fell over Grandma's lap, weeping with the relief those words gave me. My dad was still in prison. He couldn't retaliate. Couldn't put the hate in his eyes to action.

He had earned his sentence, and I had earned my freedom.

CHAPTER FORTY-NINE

NO PART of me was ready to go back to college. To face real life after pouring my heart and wounds out in front of the man who'd created both. But I couldn't stay in Woodman forever. Not with Jon a few doors down but a million miles away.

I knew I'd be back home soon. For summer break and Skye and Andrew's wedding. I couldn't believe they were actually getting married in less than two months.

I only had one stop to make before leaving town: Stormy's. I had to tell her my news in person, to see her again before the track season and semester wound down. In the last year, she'd become more than my friend; she was my rock. My *person* when Jon failed to be.

I walked up her sidewalk and knocked on the door. "Come in," she yelled.

The door was unlocked, and I pushed it open. "Where are you?"

"In here," she called from her room.

Following the sound of her voice, I found her covered in blankets, surrounded by snacks and drinks with her computer playing a movie from where it rested on her knees.

I furrowed my eyebrows. I knew she worked odd hours, but it wasn't even ten in the morning yet. Why was she still in bed?

"I'm on bed rest," she grumbled. Her voice rose to a higher octave, as if mimicking someone. "'You must keep your activity to a minimum to keep your baby girl *in there* as long as possible. Take it easy. It will be like a vacation, and the plus side is no one can ask you to do laundry!'" She rolled her eyes. "Great. Just great."

"What happened?" I asked, clearing some empty wrappers so I could sit beside her. "I just saw you Thursday and everything was fine."

She rolled her eyes back, staring at her head-board. "I tripped over a mat at work and just to be safe, Frank took me to the doctor in Austin, and that's when..." She gestured her arms around the room.

"Is your baby okay?"

"Yeah." She fiddled with her comforter. "Just at more of a risk of being born premature than she already was." Her voice rose again. "'We want to keep that bun cookin'!'"

"Your doctor did not say that."

"Yep."

"Ugh." I reached over and took a sour straw from her candy pile. The salt tanged against my tongue as I bit off a piece.

"Your turn," she said. "Distract me."

"Where should I start?" I asked. "My dad didn't get parole and Jon proposed to me."

"That did it." She sat straight up, then cringed, shifting her hips. "What happened? What did you say? How did he do it? Where's your ring?"

"Are you okay?" I asked.

"The proposal, Abi! Did he do it before or after you broke up?"

I sighed. "It's the reason why we broke up."

"What happened?"

Talking about weird maternity symptoms like we had during halftime at the game would have been preferable to reliving the proposal. But I wouldn't mind getting it off my chest. I hadn't even told Grandma all the details, but I relayed them to Stormy, hoping it would make me feel lighter somehow.

At the end of the story, I just felt more disheartened, though. "I just keep feeling guilty," I admitted. "I should have just said yes. Isn't that what marriage is? For better or worse?"

She shook her head. "You deserve *better*, *chica*. Whether it's him or someone else."

Only a month or two ago, I would have balked at the very idea that there could be someone better out there. Now, the idea just made me sad. "I couldn't imagine dating anyone else."

"Maybe Jon'll come around." She rubbed my back. "You know, everything will fall into place. Sooner or later."

"It's looking like later. Like a million years later."

She chuckled softly, which turned into a long yawn.

I stood up from her bed, making the wrappers shift and crackle.

"Where are you going?" she asked.

"You need some rest. For that bun in the oven." I

winked and tucked the blanket around her and kissed her forehead. "Call me, anytime, okay?"

She nodded. "I love you, Abi. You really do deserve the best."

For the first time, I was starting to believe it.

CHAPTER FIFTY

SURPRISINGLY, falling back into the rhythm of school and track after all that had happened was easier than I expected. Nikki and Anika made sure my evenings were filled with study sessions or date-less trips to the bars. Track kept me exhausted enough to fall asleep without too much trouble at night. Plus, we traveled to track meets, so my week-ends were full of long bus rides with the team. School kept my mind off anything else.

By the end of the semester, my grades were better than they ever had been in high school, and my track times were largely improved from the beginning of the season. Coach Cadence even said she was proud to have me on her team. But I still felt like something was missing from my life. I wasn't bullheaded enough to pretend I didn't know what, or who.

At my last session with my therapist, I admitted as much.

"Healing takes time," she said. "It took months for the flashbacks to become less frequent. Grieving a serious relationship is the same way. The important thing is that you have healthy coping mechanisms in place when those feelings become too strong."

I nodded, doubtfully mulling over the words. How long did it take to get over the love of a lifetime?

She glanced at the clock. "That's our time, but feel free to email me over the summer." She stood up and extended her hand. "It's been a pleasure working with you."

I bypassed her hand and took her in a hug. "Thank you."

As she pulled back, she straightened her outfit and nodded, a pleased smile barely masked by her placid, professional one. "Have a nice summer."

I promised her I would and left the office.

Someone exited the counselor's room across the hall at the same time, and I bumped into his chest, dropping my purse. "Oh my gosh, I'm so sorry." My eyes landed on his brace. Now I felt like an even bigger jerk. And I was thinking about Jon. Great. I tried to clear the thoughts as I picked up my bag from the ground. "I need to watch where I'm going. Are you hurt?" My throat constricted on the last word as I looked into the face of none other than Jon Scoller.

He cleared his throat, adjusting his backpack strap. "I'm fine."

"Right." I nodded and started away, swallowing down the jagged lump in my throat.

"Abi," he called.

But I kept going as fast as I could without running, until I was far away in the quad, not another person in sight.

What did it mean that Jon had been in therapy? How long had he been going?

I got out my phone to call Stormy and ask her, but a string of text messages topped my notifications.

Skye: Are you almost done, Abi? I can't wait for my bachelorette party!

Andrew: Hey, it's my party too.

Roberto: Remind me again why we're not having separate parties?

Macy: Just because you want to go to a strip club...

Leanne: It's better this way. Men going to strip clubs the night before a wedding is a chauvinistic tradition that should be put to death.

Roberto: Spare me.

Evan: Can't we all just get along?

Stormy: Maybe after a few drinks. ;)

Evan: Eyeroll emoji.

Roberto: So there will be booze? Or is that chauvi-whatever too?

Leanne: :) It's feminist approved.

Anika: Your friends are hilarious, Skye. I can see why Abi likes you guys so much.

Andrew: Are you saying we're not friends, Anika? I'm hurt.

Evan: Right? Ouch.

Roberto: Totally wounded.

I shook my head, almost fully distracted from my run-in with Jon. I looked around me at the empty campus to be sure he wasn't going the same direction, but he was nowhere to be seen.

I tapped out a response and shoved my phone in my pocket.

Abi: Finals are done and my car's already packed! Just having dinner with some friends and I'm on my way.

My drama could wait until we got home and finished the party and wedding. It was time to forget and have a good night.

Still, I dreaded saying goodbye to my track

friends. Nikki, Mollie, and Jayne had all agreed to get together with me before we went our separate ways. Nikki had to work for her dad, Mollie had an internship in Colorado, and Jayne would be going back to Sweet Water to spend the summer with her family.

As I pulled my fully packed car into a restaurant parking lot and saw my friends through the window, I realized a part of me didn't want to go home. Even though I was going to see my friends and Grandma, I was saying goodbye all over again. Maybe my heart had found another home, a new home, in these three beautiful humans. And maybe that was a good thing, because no matter where I went, I could always find a little piece of home.

CHAPTER FIFTY-ONE

ALL MY FRIENDS' cars were parked around Stormy's house. I smiled at the sight of them, feeling the pieces of my heart coming back together. I'd missed them so much, and being separated from Jon had just made me realize how much I truly needed them.

I grabbed my bag, hurried down the driveway, and burst into the house. Everyone stood around the living room, except for Stormy, who sat on the couch, her stomach protruding over a soft lap blanket.

Skye saw me first, and I launched into her arms, rocking back and forth. "You're here!"

She squeezed me back. "I missed you so much!"

"Never go to the East Coast again," I said and pulled back before moving on to Andrew, who was always at her side. "I can't believe you're getting married tomorrow."

"Me either," he said. "It's not soon enough."

Roberto pretended to gag, and that just made me want to hug him more. I squeezed him tight, realizing his body was firmer, more solid than it had been before.

"*Guera*," he said low. "College looks good on you."

My cheeks warmed. "Could say the same about the military on you."

"My turn!" Stormy yelled, pushing him aside and stretching out her arms.

I laughed, hugging her too.

I worked my way through everyone in the room, feeling more and more at peace with each embrace that passed.

"Okay," Skye said, "now that everyone's here, are we ready to go?"

"Where are we going?" I asked.

Skye turned to Stormy, who smiled deviously and said, "We're spending the night with some old friends."

That was all she would divulge, though, even with me prying every few seconds. I couldn't even guess at what she meant by old friends—I hadn't known them long enough to have a clue.

We all got into our cars and followed Frank's Suburban down the road. As we kept driving, though, my mouth fell open into an incredulous smile.

No way they were taking us here.

But then they pulled under the faded Denison Cemetery sign.

I got out of the car. "We're staying here?"

Stormy nodded proudly, hands supporting her back.

Anika nudged Skye, her mouth gaping, "Did you know about this?"

With a sheepish smile, she nodded. "I didn't want my bachelorette party to be like everyone else's."

Anika pointed at a wooden headstone. "I'd say you got your wish."

I definitely agreed, although, in a less horrified way. "Are you staying the night, Stormy?" I asked. "I thought you were on bed rest."

Frank came around the SUV with a massive air mattress and pump. "I'm on it."

"You guys are crazy," was all I could manage, shaking my head.

Evan pulled a tarp load of firewood out of his trunk, and he and Roberto got started on the fire while Leanne and Macy set up a folding table with campfire food, and Andrew and Frank set up a small tent city, Stormy's air mattress included.

Anika and I gave each other exasperated, conspiratorial looks as we helped set up all the camping chairs that had been loaded in Roberto's truck.

"And I thought Roderdale was crazy," she muttered.

I laughed. "They've got nothing on us."

Skye strung battery-powered twinkle lights on stakes around us, and as the sky went from dusk to dark, the place became even more eerily beautiful. So much so, I almost forgot we were in an abandoned cemetery.

Soon, we were all roasting hotdogs over the fire, watching them turn from pinkish brown to fully black.

"Skye," Anika asked from across the fire, "aren't you worried you'll have bags under your eyes tomorrow from sleeping out here?"

She shrugged, making her hotdog wobble. "I wasn't going to get any sleep anyway. Might as well have fun with my friends."

I smiled at her, my heart swelling and aching and tugging at the same time. She was living my fantasy —marrying the guy she loved. I couldn't help but think of Jon, asking me to marry him. Telling me he couldn't live without me. And then leaving me.

I couldn't erase the memory of his face after counseling. Drawn and surprised and...different. Yes, he was still Jon with the beautiful green eyes and the smooth skin and strong jaw. But he was thinner than before. His hair had grown out further. His shoulders seemed more...relaxed somehow.

Stormy nudged my elbow from where she lay on the air mattress. She rested on her side looking highly disgruntled. "What's with you?" she asked. "You look like you've seen a ghost."

"We're in the right place for one," I muttered.

"Seriously."

I sighed and asked Roberto to cook my food. When he agreed, I climbed onto the air mattress with Stormy. Honestly, she had the best seat in the house, under thick blankets.

"I saw Jon today," I said quietly.

"What?" Her mouth fell open. "Where?"

"At counseling," I admitted. "I ran into him on the way out."

"What did he say?"

I sighed. "Nothing. He didn't have time to."

"What do you mean?"

"I was so surprised, I just kind of ran."

She shifted, resting her head on her hand. "He didn't reach out to you after?"

"No, this is the first time I've even seen him since..."

She nodded, her wide brown eyes reflecting the fire. "Do you think he'll be at the wedding?"

My gut sank. I hadn't even thought of the possibility.

"He was invited," she said. "His parents RSVP'd. I don't know if he'll show, though."

"Has he been talking to Frank?"

She shook her head. "Frank tried calling him after it all went down, but nothing."

I tried to shake the thought of Jon at the wedding as Roberto handed me my hotdog and I started eating. Still, Jon was stuck on my heart. He always was, even when I wished, more than anything, that I could forget him.

Several hotdogs, two corn on the cobs, a s'more, and a liter of root beer later, Stormy cried, "That's it! We've got to spice up this night."

Roberto grinned across the circle at her. "You thinking what I'm thinking?"

Evan howled at the moon at the same time Andrew yelled, "STREAK!"

"Whoa, whoa, whoa!" Frank yelled. "Stormy's on bed rest. What are you thinking?"

She gave him an evil grin, to which his eyes widened, and he said, "Oh no." And she responded, "Oh yes."

That's how we all ended up running around the cemetery, half-naked, Skye in a bridal veil, the guys carrying Stormy around on an air mattress, and all of us howling at the moon.

CHAPTER FIFTY-TWO

COLD, dewy air seeped through the tent, making my skin feel sweaty and my hair curl in a weird tangle. I lifted my head from my pillow and saw the other girls stirring, their hair as messy as mine.

"Morning," Anika mumbled, looking like a zombie coming to life.

"Mmm," Skye groaned.

Stormy still snored from her spot on the air mattress. I reached over and nudged her.

"Ugh," she mumbled.

"What time is it?" I asked.

Anika held up her phone, squinting against the brightness. "Half past eight."

"We better head to Grandma's," I said. "She's expecting us at nine."

Grandma had volunteered her house for the bridal party, and even promised to keep us fed with breakfast and lunch before the ceremony at three.

I heard the boys mumbling to each other outside. I reached forward to unzip the tent, and bright light poured through the opening. After stumbling out and righting myself, I saw they'd already disassembled their tent and were working on the chairs around the campfire.

Evan saw me and lifted a hand. "Morning."

"Morning," I said, attempting to put my mess of a hair into a ponytail.

The other girls came out after me, muttering responses of their own, seeming a little worse for the wear than the guys, who looked like they'd been up and drinking coffee for hours.

Skye walked to Andrew, and he wrapped her in his arms, kissing the top of her head. I smiled at them. I couldn't believe they'd be getting married later today.

Frank dumped a chair in the bed of Roberto's truck and said, "We can take care of this if you girls wanna go into town."

We all looked at each other, and Stormy shrugged.

"Suit yourselves," she said.

Frank pointed at her.

"I know, I know," she grumbled. "Find a bed and stay there."

His pointing finger changed to a thumbs up. "Love you."

"Yeah, yeah." She walked away raising her hand in a wave.

Andrew and Skye gave each other a final, gooey goodbye before we got in our cars and left to Grandma's house.

When we walked inside, the entire place smelled like apples and cinnamon and had been decorated with white streamers and balloons.

The three women responsible stood in the kitchen: Grandma, Skye's mom, and Marta.

I stared at her, frozen by the resemblance of her green eyes to Jon's and the fact that she was even here. The last time I'd seen her, I was hearing my dad wouldn't be given parole. Watching Glen tell their son not to make things worse for me.

Her smile softened as she walked right to me and wrapped me in a hug. And then I promptly burst into tears.

The other girls seemed at a loss, but Marta rubbed my back. "Honey, it's okay."

I shook my head, sobbing for reasons I didn't completely understand and one I did. "I miss him."

She stayed silent, just kept rubbing until I finally relaxed into the tired mess I was.

The other girls tried to comfort me, but I just brushed them off. "This is Skye's day," I reminded them. "I'll be okay."

We all sat down in the living room to the cinnamon apple muffins and scrambled eggs Grandma had made for us. Gram sat beside me, pausing her meal every so often to wrap an arm around me and squeeze me tight.

No matter how much I had lost, I had her and the girls in this room. Plus the guys and my friends from college. I needed to remember that.

After breakfast, doing our hair and makeup only took so long. I liked that Skye had opted out of hiring a professional to come in and do it all. It made the day feel more relaxed than what I'd seen or heard of other weddings. To be fair, I'd only attended a handful of weddings in my life and had never actually been in one. Now that our hair and makeup were done, I wasn't sure what to do.

The other girls sprawled around the room, and Skye sat down beside me against the wall.

I rolled my head over to look at her. "How are you feeling?"

Everyone seemed to glance over at her, waiting for her answer. Skye was our friend, but so was Andrew. Her response mattered to us on so many levels.

"I'm excited," she said. "I keep feeling like all of this wedding stuff is getting in the way of what really matters."

"You're kidding," Leanne said. "I'm pretty sure my sister's watched like a million episodes of *Say Yes to the Dress* and every other wedding show on TLC."

I noted the fact that she hadn't said Denise's name. Was there a reason for that? Something I didn't know yet?

Skye shrugged. "I mean, I used to too. And maybe it would be different if we had more money." She looked down at her hands in her lap. "I feel like when you find the right guy, all of that stuff goes away."

I glanced at the engagement ring she twirled on her finger. It didn't look too different from the promise ring buried under layers of clothes in my suitcase. "How do you know you've found the right guy? How did you know to say yes?"

"It's not something that's easy to put into words,"

she said. "It's like...poetry. All the words come together in this beautiful pattern, and you don't know why these words that are matched together are any different than the millions of other words out there, but they are. They make music together, and you know that's exactly how it should be. The idea of pairing them with anything else is just...wrong."

"Exactly," Stormy said. "Like if you pulled them apart, they'd lose their meaning somehow. They make each other better."

Anika nodded. "That's how it is with Kyle. He makes me want to be better, just by being him."

Stormy propped herself up on the bed. "Before Frank, I always felt like something was missing, like I had to fill that part of myself with guys or parties or anything so I wouldn't feel that way." Her lips trembled. "He helped me stand still."

"Andrew showed me that I was enough," Skye said. "That no matter what kind of house I lived in or how my parents acted or how mean people were to me at school, I still had value. I *mattered*." She looked toward the ceiling, blinking quickly. "God, I'm going to mess up my makeup."

I put my hand on hers and managed a smile, even though my heart was splitting in two. I had all of that, those things they said, and I'd lost it. Did people get more than one piece of music in their lives? I doubted it.

Skye squeezed my hand back. "Something in him spoke to something in me and said yes long before he ever asked."

My lips faltered, and instead of facing her, I did the cowardly thing and hugged her, burying my head in her shoulder. "I'm so happy for you." And devastated for me.

Skye's mom peeked her head in the room and said we had about forty-five minutes left until we needed to leave for the church.

With her dress on, Skye was the most beautiful bride, all soft curls and bright smiles. If any marriage was going to work, it was theirs. I knew it.

We arrived at the church, and music began playing. I could hear it through the doors. Skye and her mom separated us into pairs. Evan with Anika. Frank with Stormy. Roberto with me. Macy with Leanne.

And then we walked into the church, and when I should have been seeing Andrew and the way he looked at Stormy, all I could see were those beautiful green eyes, looking right back at me.

CHAPTER FIFTY-THREE

I KEPT my eyes on Skye and Andrew, but the entire time, I could feel Jon's gaze on me. I missed him more than I dared admit. More than I dared feel, because it would *ruin* me.

How could he come here and set me back to the first day he left with a single look? Months of trying to be on my own, of focusing on my friends, of pouring myself into track and school...and I was back where I'd begun.

Only this time, I couldn't remember why we'd parted. Couldn't remember how I'd ever let our circumstances tear me away from the love of my life.

The pastor's words caught my attention, and I held on to each one.

"There will be times when it seems like every-

thing is going against you as a couple," he said.
"There will be financial setbacks, illnesses, injuries,
family drama, children, parents, lost jobs, and
anything you can imagine in between. That's when
you cling to each other. That's when you hold on.
That's when you fight with everything you have and
say no to anything that is not each other. And you
keep saying no, because today, you said yes. You said
I choose you."

I watched Andrew's mouth form the words to
Skye, *I choose you*, and my heart swelled for them
and shattered for me, for all I'd lost. If I had it to do
all over again, I'd stop Jon in the hallway and tell him
I *chose* him. I'd fight for him when he'd lost the fight
for himself.

But I couldn't go back. I could only go forward.

And right now, that looked like cheering for my
friends as they slipped rings on each other's fingers
and sealed their promise with the most important
kiss of their lives.

We followed them out of the church, under
showers of rice, and went to take pictures. There was
a jittery excitement in the air, like the moment they'd
been waiting for their entire lives had finally come to
fruition.

With the photographer's direction, we smiled for

photo after photo under a nearby oak tree. Skye and Andrew made a beautiful couple. I couldn't wait to see the pictures. I tried to focus on them and their happiness through the pictures and the beginning of the reception, but with the cake cut and the first dances done, I was running out of things to distract myself.

The love and the loss of my life was here. I'd spotted him sitting at a table at the far end of the room. His tie was loosened. His long hair hung around his face, smooth and edgy. Different but the same. My heart was torn between wanting to see him and knowing that if I did, I wouldn't be able to recover.

Not that this was recovery. My shaking hands and pounding heart and constantly being afraid to look in his direction for fear of what I'd find, but looking anyway because I couldn't peel my eyes away.

The mother-son dance started, and Grandma came to the bridal table. "May I have this dance?"

I turned my gaze away from Jon gently swaying with his mom.

"Are you sure?" I asked.

She nodded. "It was this one or the daddy-daughter dance, and, well, I like this song better."

My eyebrows came together. "Really?" They were both sappy country songs.

"Yes, now hurry up and get down here." She wiggled her fingers impatiently. "We're going to miss it."

When I stepped off the platform and joined her on the dance floor, she held my hands and gently spun me in what I guessed was a waltz. I might be able to outrun my grandma now, but there was no way I could out-dance her.

I tried to stick to the opposite side of the dance floor from Jon, but soon I heard his voice.

"You're supposed to let me lead, Mom," he said.

She chuckled. "Old habits."

My back bumped into someone.

"Oh, sorry, Marta," Grandma said. "Clumsy me."

I glanced from Jon to Marta to Grandma, my mouth open. I knew exactly what was happening. "You're a terrible actor," I told Grandma.

Grandma flung her hands up. "Well, what else were we supposed to do? This is ridiculous." She gestured between Jon and me. "You're both clearly miserable. Talk to each other."

Marta nodded. "You've been separated long enough."

Jon looked to me, his green eyes full of...something. I couldn't tell what. And that hurt even worse because I used to know him as well as I knew myself. But now...

"Excuse me," I said and walked away. Every second that passed made oxygen harder and harder to get.

I skirted the room and made a beeline to the bathrooms. High school had familiarized me with seeking shelter in a bathroom stall. Time to go back to an old favorite.

When I walked in, Stormy stood at the sink, staring in the mirror, and breathing deeply.

"You're not going to beli—" I gave her a confused look. "What are you doing?"

And then I stepped in water. "Gross. Is one of the toilets leaking?"

She stared straight back at me. "That's my water."

CHAPTER FIFTY-FOUR

MY HEART FROZE somewhere between my stomach and the floor. "Wh-what?"

She pointed at her stomach. "I'm going into labor."

"Oh my God," I cried. "How long do we have?"

Exasperated, she said, "The doctor didn't exactly give me a countdown timer!"

"Okay, okay." I tried to breathe deeply, letting my athlete instincts take over. "Okay, I'll go get your mom and Frank. You go to my car." I grabbed my clutch and handed her the keys, thanking my lucky stars I'd brought my car earlier in the day so I'd have it. "Sit in the back seat."

She stood still though, her eyes full of fear. "Abi, I'm two weeks early."

I put my hands on her shoulders. "She's right on time. It will be okay."

With a nod, she hurried from the bathroom, and I walked back to the reception, trying to hide the pounding of my heart in my chest. I found Frank at the punch table, about to pour himself a glass.

"Stormy's going into labor," I whispered in Frank's ear, and his entire face went white.

He set down his drink. "Where is she?"

"My car." I told him where it was parked. "I'm going to get her mom. We'll meet you at the hospital."

"She has to deliver in Austin," he said.

"We'll meet you there then." Just as he was about to walk away, I grabbed his arm and smiled. "Congratulations."

He gave me a grin before hurrying away.

I found Stormy's mom next, and the second I told her, her eyes lit with excitement. "Stormy's having her baby."

Feeling her giddiness, I nodded. "I'll meet you in the parking lot. I just have to tell Skye first."

She agreed, and I went straight to Skye and Andrew where they spun slow circles on the dance floor. I hurriedly told them the news. "I'm sorry I have to go, but congratulations. Really, I'm so happy for you two."

"Hold up," Skye said, stopping me.

"What?" I asked, turning back. I hoped she wasn't upset.

She looked the opposite. "There's no way we're not going to be there."

"It's your wedding," I said.

She met Andrew's eyes, and he walked straight for the DJ's stand. After taking the microphone, he said, "Sorry, folks, but I've got to get my girl home. Enjoy the dance. I'll see you later!"

Applause sounded as our group of friends fled the reception and started toward the parking lot. Wedding or not, this baby was coming.

* * *

When we finally got inside the hospital, they had already brought Stormy to the delivery room.

Andrew and Skye went to the waiting room while Stormy's mom and I headed for the maternity ward. I wanted to rush inside Stormy's room, where I could hear her crying on the other side of the door, but a nurse blocked us.

"Two people at a time," she said.

Stormy's mom went in first, and after a long moment, she came back out. "Take care of my girl," she whispered and hugged me tight.

"I will," I promised.

After she let me go, I rushed to Stormy's side and took her hand. "What's going on?"

"My blood pressure's too high. The baby's breech. They're thinking about doing a cesarean, but my doctor isn't here yet."

I gripped her hand harder. "What can I do?"

She clenched her teeth and breathed deep. This must have been a contraction.

Frank squeezed her other hand, agony clear on his face. He hated seeing her in pain. His expression only evened when she loosened her grip and breathed normally again.

"You're doing enough," she finally said, weak. "I'm glad you're here."

"Me too."

I looked down at our hands. Hers were paler than her usual olive tint, but her fingernails stood out with a pretty red shade of polish.

What seemed like hours passed just like that. Riding out contractions together while nurses came in and out, updating us on the status of Stormy's blood pressure and dilation.

"I can't just *lie* here forever," she announced after the latest check.

Frank sat up in his chair. "You'll get to leave once we have the baby."

Stormy rolled her eyes. "First of all, I'll be the one *having* the baby. Second, I meant right now. What am I supposed to do? Twiddle my thumbs? Play mercy with Abi?"

I shrugged. "It wouldn't feel right fighting a pregnant lady."

"See?" She gestured at me. "Boring. What should we do?"

An impish grin covered Frank's face. "Want to streak again? I can roll this bed around a hell of a lot easier than I could carry that air mattress."

"God no," she laughed. "All the staff would pass out before they needed to deliver the baby."

"Exactly," I added. "And it would be disgraceful to streak in a hospital. That's just something we do over dead bodies, right?"

Stormy laughed, then clutched my arm. "You're going to make me pee my pants."

I stifled a laugh. "Frank, I think I found our game."

His eyebrow quirked. "See who can make her pee the bed first?"

"I hate you," she said, barely hiding her smile.

"Hey, Frank," I said. "What's the difference between a pregnant lady and a lightbulb?"

Stormy dragged her hand over her face.

"I don't know, Abi. What is it?" Frank asked, the perfect partner in crime.

"You can unscrew a lightbulb."

He guffawed while Stormy gave me a well-humored glare. "You're going to have to do better than that."

"Let me try," Frank said. "There was a priest, a rabbi, and a—"

A woman in the doorway wearing hospital scrubs cleared her throat, smiling. "I hate to interrupt the punchline, but I think it's time for this baby to come."

I moved out of the way so she could talk with Stormy. I picked up pieces of the conversation, but most of it went over my head. I understood the important parts though. Stormy would have a C-section with one guest in the operating room, meaning I would have to wait with the others.

While the doctor left to the operating room and nurses came in to move her, I went to Stormy's side and held her hand. In her hospital bed, surrounded by white and mint-green bedding, Stormy looked so small, even with her bump creating a mound under the blankets. Her eyes met mine, wide, afraid.

I wanted to comfort her, but I was having a hard time doing it without breaking down. I was scared too. For her and the baby.

"Do you remember your first day in Woodman?" she asked.

Didn't we have more important things to do than walk down memory lane? But I humored her. "What about it?"

"I probably came on a little strong."

I snorted. "Understatement of the century."

A smile crossed her face. "Yeah, well...I'm glad you came. Because if you hadn't fallen for Jon and the guys hadn't told me what an ass I was being, I wouldn't have stopped chasing Jon and let Frank in."

Frank's eyes met mine, and a corner of his lips lifted. An unspoken thank you.

"And look at us now," Stormy said, turning her eyes lovingly on him before looking back to me. "We're having a baby. You're going to be the godmother. Life is so different."

An ache stabbed at my chest. Normally, Stormy would have been the first person I went to about my grandma's surprise ambush and how much I still missed Jon, but I couldn't tell her right now. This was her night. My godchild's night.

She squeezed my hand, her eyes knowing what I couldn't bring myself to say. "It's crazy how things work out."

I wiped at my eyes and blinked quickly. "You're going to do great," I said, my voice thick. Then I met Frank's eyes. "Frank's here for you, and your mom and I will be right outside." I brushed her hair back. "I can't wait to meet your baby."

She managed a smile, and that was the last I saw of her before they wheeled her bed out of the room.

CHAPTER FIFTY-FIVE

I FOUND her mom in the waiting room, tapping into her phone. Stormy's stepdad sat with her, along with all of our friends in their wedding attire.

Her mom stood up. "How is she? The baby's not here yet, is she?"

I shook my head. "They're taking her back for a C-section." I repeated all the medical jargon I'd heard the doctor tell Stormy, thinking it would probably mean more to an actual mom than me.

She nodded, a worried look still on her face. She looked so much like Stormy with her eyebrows furrowed like that.

"Can I get you anything?" I asked. "Coffee? Water? Food?" Moving had to be better than sitting here, waiting for answers.

"Good luck." Her husband folded his arms across his chest. "She won't let me help at all."

With a quick shake of her head and an apologetic smile, she said, "I wouldn't be able to keep anything down anyway."

I understood. Without Stormy's reassurance, I would have been falling apart right now. I had no idea what Stormy would do if the baby wasn't okay. What I'd do if Stormy wasn't.

I dropped into the open seat next to Skye. She took my hand and held it on her lap. I squeezed it back.

"How are you doing, Abi?" she asked quietly. "I saw Jon there."

I couldn't lie. But I also couldn't wallow. I needed to be here for Stormy. "I've had better days. But I don't want to talk about me." I turned to Stormy's mom. "How long does a cesarean usually take? I want to see this baby!"

Excitement rose to the surface of her face. "Me too. I think it should be an hour, tops, once they get started."

I glanced at the clock on the wall. "What time did I come out here?"

"Around eight, I think."

The minute hand was somewhere around the thirty mark. "Thirty more minutes?"

She nodded. "Thirty more minutes and I'll be a grandma."

Her husband rubbed her back. "You're going to spoil that baby rotten."

"Damn straight." Then she leaned over and gave him a kiss.

I smiled at the two of them. They were sweet. So was the couple on my other side. Now I knew why Roberto complained so much about being surrounded by couples. I had to move, to get the adrenaline and pain out of my system.

"I'll be back," I said.

Evan got up and walked with me. After we got out of hearing distance, he said, "It's tense in there."

I nodded, even though that wasn't why I needed to leave.

"You looked beautiful today," he said.

I managed a smile and nodded at his suit. "You clean up nice yourself."

He pulled at his lapels. "I do, don't I?"

A small laugh escaped my chest. I felt lighter already. "I needed to get some air."

He nodded, hearing the words I didn't say, and

put his arm around me. We walked the halls, my heels' clack against the tile echoing off the walls, until it got closer to an hour. We got back to the waiting room just in time to see Frank in a surgical gown and a face mask around his neck saying, "Violeta is here. Five pounds, six ounces, and seventeen inches long."

Tears pooled in Stormy's mom's eyes. "A little girl."

"Congratulations, man," Evan said.

"Is she healthy?" I asked. "Is Stormy okay?"

"Yes and yes," Frank said. "They're in recovery now if you'd like to see them."

Stormy's mom and I were past him before he even finished his sentence.

"It's that way!" he called behind us.

After we changed directions, we finally found the recovery room where a nurse was working with the tiniest baby I'd ever seen.

Stormy's mom went right to her daughter, while I ventured toward the baby, trying to understand how my heart could immediately love something so small that looked exactly like Frank.

I wiped at my face and found moisture there. "Oh, Stormy," I said. "She's precious."

"Just like her mom," Stormy's mother said.

The nurse finished and wrapped Violeta up. "Would you like to hold her?"

I looked to Stormy for permission, and she nodded.

"Yes," I said, still unsure. "Will I break her?"

The nurse chuckled. "You'll do fine." She transferred the bundle to my arms.

Violeta was incredibly light, even swaddled in blankets. Her eyes were closed, but I could hear her breathing along with the monitors in the room.

"Hi, precious girl," I breathed. "I'm your godmother, Abi, and I'm here for you no matter what." I turned to Stormy so I could look at her. "You know your mom, she's my best friend. You are going to love being her daughter. She's the best person I know." My throat constricted. "I wouldn't be here without her, and I'll never be thankful enough to know her."

I met Stormy's eyes and saw they were just as wet as mine. "I love you," I mouthed to her and passed Violeta to her grandmother.

I was just a part of her story, and she was an uncharacteristically bright part of mine.

I left the room to give someone else a turn and walked right into the last person I'd expected to see.

CHAPTER FIFTY-SIX

I STARED AT JON. That was I all I could do.

He glanced around us, at our friends trying to hide their intrigue. "Can we talk?"

My mouth worked, but no words came out.

"Come on." He took my hand, such a familiar gesture that memories and warmth and hurt and loss came flooding back with all the force of a tidal wave, ready to sweep me under the surface and bury me forever.

Wordlessly, I followed him, was swept away, until we reached an empty hallway with abandoned beds lining the hall.

Finally, I found my vocal cords. "Jon, what are you doing here?"

He held my hand with both of his, meeting my

eyes and then looking down. His hair fell into his eyes, and he swept it to the side.

"Abi, I..." His words failed him just as mine had earlier, and he stepped back, raking his hands through his hair. "God, I've planned what I would say, I swear I have, but..." He looked at me, then turned away.

I reached out to him and took his hand. "Then let me."

His eyes found mine, green, hurting, scared. "I didn't want it to be this way. It was going to be better, but then you left the reception, and I couldn't stand the thought of seeing you walk away again."

I pressed a finger to his lips. "Can I?"

He nodded but reached up and held my hand.

I melted into the warmth, into his strength, because I needed it.

"Jon, I'm sorry."

"I'm sorry."

I shook my head. "I am. I leaned on you, depended on you, needed you to be my rock. I never knew how hard it was to be that for someone until..." I glanced at his leg, brace-free but not without its wounds. "I've thought about it, you, every single day. About how I could have done better, supported you better, but I'm just as lost as I was then."

He held my hands to his chest. I felt the rising and falling of his breath. Knew his heart lay right under the spot where my hands touched his shirt.

"Maybe..." He paused. "Maybe it's like the pastor said. That we needed to choose each other. And I chose the pain. But I'm not going to do that anymore."

I blinked up at him. "What are you saying?"

"Abi, I'm saying I'm ready. You deserved a better man than I could be, and I worked, God, I've worked to be that man. I've been in counseling. I focused on my grades, doubled down on PT. I'm ready, but that doesn't matter if you're not ready to give me another chance. I know I don't deserve it."

"You don't," I agreed, tears flooding my eyes. "You have no idea how much you hurt me. But it doesn't matter what you deserve, because I want you. I want you every day, through every heartache, through every test and trial and wedding reception interrupted by my best friend's baby." I let out a watery laugh, and he wiped at my eyes.

"Are you saying what I think you're saying?" he asked.

"Jon." I reached up and held his face in my hands. "Will you marry me?"

He crushed me to his chest, faster than I could

have ever imagined, holding me tight like he could make up for the days, weeks, and months we'd missed each other. "Yes," he said. And he held me even tighter.

But I needed even more of him. I found his lips with mine and kissed every breath of mine into his. Every cell of mine into his. Because I was his. From the first day I'd met him. From the first time I'd learned I couldn't live without him. From now until forever.

CHAPTER FIFTY-SEVEN
THREE MONTHS LATER

I STARTED down the aisle holding a simple, blush-colored bouquet. Plenty of people filled the chairs at the end—friends, family, a few people I didn't even recognize. I kept my eyes down on the grass of the Scollers' back lawn as I walked. I'd hate to trip and embarrass myself.

When I reached the end and finally looked up, Jorge smiled at me. I returned a reassuring grin of my own before turning to see my grandma. She was stunning in a light blue suit, holding a bouquet of her own. Her hair curled softly around her cheeks, loose and down instead of up in its usual bun. At first, she smiled at the crowd around her, like she was embarrassed they had all come for her, but then she only had eyes for Jorge.

His shoulders straightened and his eyes watered as she walked toward him, full of pride and emotion I couldn't quite describe. Grandma's lips pulled in a trembling smile, and the expression brought tears to my own eyes. This was her happily ever after, all over again.

I might have suffered my own personal tragedy, but Grandma hadn't been let off easy. Between losing her husband, having her daughter put in jail, and then taking on her granddaughter, I admired how strong she'd been through it all. That she'd still been soft enough to open hear heart to love.

I glanced at Jon where he sat with his parents in the front row. We'd finally learned to do the same, to love each other and be soft through the hard times.

When Grandma reached me, she hugged me and handed me her bouquet. I held both and listened as the ceremony began. It was different. Unlike Skye and Andrew, who'd just been starting their journey, Grandma and Jorge knew what it meant to be married. Knew how to love wholly and commit to another person.

"The question," the preacher said, "is if you can do it again. If you'll be able to join fully to one another in what is left of this amazing life, and love like there's no time left. You both know we're not promised anything beyond today. Will you make it count?"

I couldn't help it. I looked at Jon. How stupid we'd been to part, not once but twice. To think that shouldering a burden alone would somehow spare the other. We were linked. In this incredible life, we didn't have time to waste learning that lesson again.

His eyes told me he felt exactly the same way.

Grandma and Jorge exchanged "I do's" and then we began the dance. The Scollers had rented a wooden dance floor for the reception, and I sat at the wedding party's table while Grandma and Jorge began their first dance.

With my chin resting on my folded hands, I watched them slowly turn in circles, every bit as in love as Skye and Andrew were on their day. Stormy was here somewhere, with Violeta. I smiled, thinking this was my goddaughter's second wedding.

"You look happy."

I turned to see Jon smiling at me.

"Hey, you," I said. I reached for his hand. "It was good, don't you think?"

"It was amazing." He squeezed my fingers and sat down in the chair next to me. Tucking a piece of hair behind his ear, he said, "But the girl next to your grandma stole the show."

"Oh?" I quirked an eyebrow.

"Yeah." He scratched his neck. "I mean, I hate to say it, but I couldn't take my eyes off her."

My cheeks warmed. "Yeah?"

"Definitely." His fingers traced a pattern on my bare shoulder as he moved my hair back. When his eyes met mine, there was so much feeling in them, I had no idea what to do.

"Jon?"

He took my hand and looked down. "We were so stupid. I was stupid."

I reached for his chin and held his face in my hands. "I don't want to waste today feeling bad about yesterday."

He nodded.

Leaning forward, I placed a kiss on his cheek. It was warm under my lips.

"I got something for you," he said.

I bumped my knee against his. "You know, you're supposed to get the bride and groom a present on the wedding day."

"Ah." He pretended to be regretful. "I told you, you stole the show."

I rolled my eyes.

"Well, I guess I could wait..."

"No way." I stuck out my hand. "Show me."

Jon reached into his pocket and placed a delicate silver ring in the palm of my hand, and my mouth fell open. "Grandma's ring?"

His eyes searched me, gauging my reaction. "What do you think?"

"I..." Why wouldn't my words come? I touched the stone and the smooth edges of the circle. "Grandpa gave this to her. They were nineteen."

"As old as we are."

I looked at him, confused. "How did you know?"

He glanced at Grandma, who had broken her bubble with Jorge to send us an approving smile.

"Grandma told you?"

He nodded, taking the ring and moving my hand, slowly slipping it on my finger.

"She said your grandpa got down on one knee, opened a box with this ring in it, and said 'You'd be crazy to say yes, but will you?'"

A small laugh escaped my parted lips, even though tears were forming in my eyes.

"I know you asked me, and I already said yes, but it's not because I'm crazy." He reached up and ran his hand over my hair, tucked it back behind my shoulder again. "It's because I'm not. Saying yes to you was the easiest decision I've ever made."

I held my hand to my chest, the ring and all its

years of love under my palm. "Have I mentioned I love you?"

He brought his forehead to mine, closing his eyes. "And I love you."

There, in his parents' backyard, with my grandma dancing with the love of her life, I realized my home had been here all along. In the heart of the boy next door.

I hated moving. With a passion. But we were finally back in Woodman. Back home.

I dumped a box of Jon's social work textbooks he refused to get rid of in the guest room and stood up to wipe my forehead. A stinging sensation spread, and I jerked my hand away. This damn, beautiful diamond ring had scratched me. I needed to be more careful.

A shutter sounded, and a flash of light filled the room.

I jerked upright and saw Grandma holding up the digital camera we'd gotten her for her birthday. "You scared the crap out of me, Gram!"

She focused on the screen and then turned it so I could see the most hideous photo ever taken of me. "One for the newlyweds' family album," she said.

"Uh huh," I said. "Sure."

"I would help with unpacking, but…" She shrugged from the old chair she sat on surrounded by boxes and flipped to the next page of her magazine. "I guess I'm too old."

I rolled my eyes at her smug smile and left the room. Only half the trailer to go.

Evan peered at me from behind a box. "Where do you want this?"

Making out Jon's chicken scratch was near impossible. "It either says kazoo or…kitchen."

"I'll put it in the kazoo then."

Laughing, I passed him and Frank and Roberto until I got back outside. Thank goodness the girls were in the kitchen unpacking because I could see how this moving thing could quickly become a weeks-long ordeal now that I actually owned a few things.

Jon stood with his dad in the trailer, arguing over what should come out first in the Jenga-pile of furniture they'd loaded up.

When he caught my gaze, he said, "I'm taking a break," and jumped out. It was almost easy to forget he was ever injured now. "Please tell me we have some water left in the cooler."

"Yeah." I nodded and started back toward the porch. Off to the side, by the porch swing, we had a blue cooler full of drinks for everyone who'd come to help.

After I picked a couple of bottles out and handed one to him, he sat back on the swing, and I flopped down beside him. I rested my head on his shoulder, not caring how sweaty it was.

"Whose idea was it to move in the middle of August?" I asked.

"I don't know, but we should take away their sunscreen."

"You wouldn't dare." I laughed and looked up at him. He'd been growing out his facial hair. I liked him clean-shaven, but this was nice too. More mature.

"At least we have a little time to get unpacked before I start my job."

With half a smile, I nodded. It would be nice to keep him from commuting an hour or more every day, depending on his caseload. I was afraid of finishing my program online though. School had never been my strong suit. Was I really cut out for the hours of solo studying it would take to get my law degree and pass the bar?

"Get out of your head," he said. "You're going to do great."

"How do you always know what I'm thinking?"

"We've been together too long."

I shook my head. "Five years is not too long."

"Neither is forever." He smiled at me, his eyes soft, his lips...

I pressed my own to his. Perfectly kissable.

When we parted, he stared over the grassy front lawn. "What's next?"

"Maybe the couch?"

"No." He shook his head and locked his beautiful green eyes on mine, all humor gone from his expression. "For us?"

Flutters started low in my stomach and rose through my chest. We had nothing but time—forever. A home with extra bedrooms. A fenced-in backyard. Careers. Plans. I bit my lip, knowing what was left.

I'd dreamed of having a child. One who looked exactly like Jon, with bright green eyes and a smile that could instantly melt anyone's heart. I hoped they'd have his laugh and his sense of humor and his heart for others. But now something deeper called to me.

I bit my lip. "What if we adopt?"

His eyes flared open. "Really?"

I nodded. "I want to do for someone else what Gram did for me. I want to give them a home." I squeezed his hand. "A family."

He reached out and brushed his thumb over my cheek. "I love your heart. I couldn't think of anything better."

"Are we ready?" I asked.

He pulled me close and held me to his side. "With you? I'm ready for anything. Everything."

Him sitting next to me was already *everything*. But maybe I could live with a little bit more of forever, whatever it would bring.

Thank you for reading the final book of Abi's story. To stay in her world just a little longer, get the FREE story of her and Jon's wedding today!

Use this QR code to get the free story!

Keep turning the page to get a preview of Curvy Girls Can't Date Quarterbacks, the first book in my body positive romance series called the Curvy Girl Club!

Use this code to discover Curvy Girls Can't Date Quarterbacks!

CURVY GIRLS CAN'T DATE QUARTERBACKS

CHAPTER ONE

WHY WAS I taking a pregnancy test as a virgin? Oh yeah, my mom was literally insane.

I brought the stick with the words flashing *not pregnant* to the dining room, where my mom, dad, and brother sat with their ridiculous grapefruit breakfasts. It landed with a satisfying clack next to the pile of papers my mom was grading.

"Can we please move on?" I asked, hands on hips. "I've already told you I'm not dating anyone."

She pushed her reading glasses up her nose and held the stick out so the results could come into focus before sighing and setting it on the table. "Rory, you've missed three periods in a row and you don't want to go on birth control. *And* you've gained ten pounds in the last three months. You can't blame me for being suspicious."

Dad nearly choked on his grapefruit and swallowed a big gulp of water, choking more.

My brother looked way too pleased at all of this. As a boy, a junior in high school, and a ridiculously fit runner, he usually got off easy from all of Mom's "self-improvement" rampages. From college plans to weight loss, I'd heard it all.

Sometimes, having a mom who was also a health teacher sucked. Hard. "Glad to know you're keeping track of my cycles, Mom."

"Someone needs to." She drew a big red smiley face on a paper next to a fifty percent. For Mom's class, that was a pretty good grade.

"Mom," I said. "Look at me." I gestured at my size 1X school uniform and the required navy blue socks that strained at my calves. "I'm a virgin. I've told you that. So unless an angel shows up tonight and tells me I'm carrying the second son of God, you can give the pregnancy stuff a rest."

Dad nearly choked again, but Mom ignored him and gave me an *almost* abashed smile as she held the stick back out to me. "Okay, but I still want Dr. Edmonson to get you checked out."

I turned my eyes toward the ceiling, contemplating my next move. Knowing arguing would be futile, just as it had been when she'd presented me with the test this morning, I gave in. "When is the appointment?"

"How do you know I already scheduled it?"

My dad, brother, and I each gave her a look, and she glanced up from her papers to show a sheepish smile. "This morning, at eight."

"So, I'm missing first period," I complained. Not that I was super into math, but I could have aced any test on the back of Beckett Langley's head. "I thought you were worried about me missing periods?"

She ignored my comment completely. "I'll talk to Mr. Aris, and Dr. Edmonson will have you done in time for you to be back for health class!" She flashed me a grin, standing up with her plate. "Now, hurry up and eat your breakfast. You're going to be late."

Keeping my grumblings to myself, I sat in front of half a grapefruit and thought of all the things I could do with this stupid spoon that didn't involve shoving the bitter pink flesh down my throat. Smashing this pregnancy test was high on the list, as was wiping the smirk from my brother's face.

I glared at him. "Don't you have a jock convention to be at?"

His smirk grew wider as he came and gave me a kiss on the cheek. "Love you, sis. Glad you're not pregnant. But then again, I would have made a great uncle."

"Yeah, yeah," I said, stabbing my spoon into the grapefruit. "Love you, too." At least since I was driving myself to the doctor's appointment, I could make a quick fast-food stop on the way and be rid of the evidence before I made it to school.

Dad wiped his mouth with a napkin. "I better get going too." He stood and kissed my cheek. "Let me know how the appointment goes."

"Sure," I said, toying with the pulp at the end of my spoon. I tried a bite, but I just couldn't stomach it.

Giving up on "breakfast," I got up from the table. After slipping on my dress-code-compliant loafers, I grabbed my keys from the hooks by the door. Usually, I rode with Mom and Aiden, so at least this appointment gave me the chance to get my car out on the road. A mix between sensible and sporty, my Audi was the coolest thing about me.

I hit the road and stopped at my favorite drive-thru before going to my mandated appointment at RWE Medical.

I walked through the sliding doors and gave Betty, the receptionist, a pained smile.

"Mom sent you in again?" she asked.

"Yup," I said, switching my paper bag to the other hand so I could sign in.

"An eight-a-m-er, no less. Nice." She pushed some curly hair over her shoulder and typed in my name and date of birth without having to ask for it. "Sign this, and the nurse will be out to grab ya soon."

I scribbled my name on the scuffed digital pad and sat down in one of the plush leather chairs. Hints of breakfast wafted from the paper bag in my hand, making my mouth water. The only other thing that made me drool this much was Beckett's perfectly messy hair and his muscled shoulders. How he managed to look like a prep-school god in his uniform while I looked like an overweight Mia Thermopolis—pre-princess makeover—I had no idea.

I got the breakfast sandwich out of my bag and took a bite, savoring the sausage. My eyes slid closed. So much better than a grapefruit.

So much better.

"Hey, Rory," a voice said beside me.

A sexy voice.

I gulped down my bite and, brushing biscuit

crumbs from my lips, turned to see the deepest hazel eyes.

Beckett Langley knew my name?

"Beckett," I breathed, then coughed and said his name at a normal tone like I wasn't a complete love-struck psychopath. "Beckett. What—um, what are you doing here?"

Okay, not a perfect second attempt, but closer.

He sank back in the leather chair next to mine and held up his arm sporting a black wrist brace. "Fell wrong in practice. Coach wants an x-ray before he'll let me play again."

"Oh," I said, completely distracted by him. Now that I had looked away from his eyes, I couldn't stop taking in the rest of him. The tight Emerson Academy t-shirt and mesh shorts that hung on his muscular legs. The dampness of his hair that made it look almost black.

"What about you?" he asked.

"Oh, um." God, could I stop saying um? But then again, it was better than the whole pregnancy-test-missing-periods-virgin conversation we could be having...

"Rory?" Chloe said by the door. She was wearing Winnie the Pooh scrubs today, and I'd never been more grateful to see Pooh.

"That's me," I said, half to her and half to Beckett.

He gave me a two-finger salute. "See you in math tomorrow, Rory."

I nearly choked on my saliva. He knew my name *and* that we were in math together? "I—um—yeah."

I bunched up the paper bag with my food and stood up, straightening my shirt—and checking for stray crumbs.

As I walked to meet Chloe and go back for my appointment, I felt Beckett's eyes on my back... and my heart in my throat.

Between the blood test, an ultrasound (that went where no man had ever gone before), and a massive list of probing—er—intrusive questions, I was done. More than done. And, for the first time in my life, I was glad to be wearing my school uniform again.

A knock sounded on the door. "Decent?"

"Yes," I managed, and Dr. Edmonson came in.

I got a great view of his bald patch as he walked through the door, flipping through my charts.

"It's what I expected." He sighed, every bit as dramatic but nowhere near as sigh-worthy as McDreamy.

"What is it?" I asked. "Because I'd love to get my mom to stop bombarding me with pregnancy tests."

He chuckled, but quickly sobered. "Usually, we'd wait for the readings to come back, but as a favor to your mom, I took a peek myself. You have PCOS." At my confused look, he added, "Polycystic ovarian syndrome."

For the next fifteen minutes, he explained this thing I had no idea existed but had somehow taken over my body, my weight, and apparently my fertility. He explained why I'd packed on the pounds so quickly since middle school and had to go to weekly waxing appointments with my mother. That I'd have a harder time conceiving, when the time came, if I was able to at all.

All of it seemed overwhelming. And unfair. I mean, yeah, I ate fast food, but so did half the kids at Emerson Academy. Why was I the one ballooning out and they could still stay in single-digit uniforms and procreate like monkeys? "So, how do we get rid of it?"

"You could try to lose weight."

I rested back in my chair and rolled my eyes. "My mom's on that one." Everyone acted like if you were fat, all your medical problems were fat. They never wanted to look beyond the extra layer of tissue to see what was really going on.

"I'm assuming she doesn't know about that." He sent a pointed look to my takeout bag, and I scooted it behind my backpack.

I refused to respond. That was his only solution? Try to do something my mom and I had been working at for months? You'd think years in med school would have given him some advanced thinking skills, but apparently not.

"Maybe you should take her advice," Dr. Edmonson said. "In the meantime, I'm prescribing you birth control to help balance out your hormones and jump-start your cycles. You'll be feeling better in no time."

I wanted to tell him I felt just fine. That aside from my weight, I led a perfectly average existence no one could shake a stick at. Whatever that phrase meant. Plus, not having the bloody devil staining my underwear and stomping on my uterus every month wasn't the worst thing ever.

"Now, I promised your mother I'd have you done in time for class." He looked at me over his spectacles. "Don't make me break her promise."

I turned and grabbed my bag. "We wouldn't want that, now would we?"

My lips quickly fell as I walked out of the office.

Any dreams I'd had of Beckett knowing my name and holding a secret torch for me shattered as I processed the news. How could I be worrying about infertility before I'd even hit second base? And this disease meant I would have a harder time losing weight, but that was my only chance at being healthy? It didn't make any sense.

I got into my car and slammed the gearshift into reverse. What kind of cruel joke was this? What had I done to deserve this? I had straight As. I volunteered. I tutored every now and then. Heck, I even ate my mom's stupid grapefruit. None of it mattered. None of it made a difference.

I was still fuming when I parked next to Merritt Alexander's stupid hot-pink Hummer and walked into Emerson Academy. The school's motto over the entranceway mocked me. *Ad Meliora.* Toward better things.

Or more tortuous things. Like an hour-long lecture presented by my very own mother on menstrual cycles and condoms and STIs.

I rolled my eyes before opening the classroom door. If only Mom didn't have Dr. Edmonson in her back pocket, I could have stalled and gotten out of there in time for lunch. Doctors were notoriously slow.

Most of the girls in health class already lounged in their seats, but we had a few minutes before the hour started. Mom rose from her desk and came to me.

"Any news?" she asked quietly.

"It's…" I looked away from her, toward the board where the projector had the first lesson slide on the pull-down screen. My mouth hung open at the four letters on the title slide.

"What?" She followed my eyes. "Oh, yeah, should be a good discussion for you girls."

"No, I—"

The bell shrilled, and she rubbed a hand on my shoulder. "Catch me at lunch so you can tell me what Dr. Edmonson said?"

Deftly, I nodded and went to the open seat in the front row where I sat in Mom's class. Every class except math, to be fair. Mom would know before I did if I'd been goofing off or not paying attention. Perks of having a parent for a teacher.

Mom began the lecture, reading from the slides and covering all the information I'd just learned from Dr. Edmonson.

"Some common symptoms are hair growth on the upper lip, weight gain, especially around your middle, and irregular cycles..." Her mouth went slack, and she turned her eyes on me.

I nodded.

She swallowed.

I felt the entire class's eyes on me.

"Excuse me," she said to the class. "I have to make a call. Work on...something until I get back."

She left to a chorus of murmurs, and I tried to hide my red cheeks. She hadn't pointed me out directly, but she might as well have.

"This is so dumb," Merritt trilled from the back row where she sat with the rest of her groupies. "Mrs. H. might as well just give another lecture on 'the dangers of obesity.'"

Her friend Tinsley made an ominous "ooooh" sound like the ghost of Christmas Fat was haunting the room.

Poppy giggled, egging them on, as usual.

"I don't get it," Merritt continued. "Why not just cut the Twinkies and quit whining about it?"

I gritted my teeth and turned to see how Jordan, the scholarship student sitting next to me, was reacting to this. She weighed at least as much as me. But her eyes were on her homework assignment, even though her hand wasn't writing.

Tinsley scoffed, "I mean, I'd trade Twinkies for not being fat any day."

Merritt's voice turned falsely pensive. "I don't know. I mean, it's one thing to have a little extra cushion, but another to be *obese*."

"True," Poppy said.

Was Zara hearing this? If anyone would stand up to Merritt, it would be her—she was my size but had curves in the right places—and a feisty personality to match. Plus, her dad was rich enough to have as much clout as Merritt's parents. I turned to see if she was catching it, but she kept her thumbs tapping over her phone. Probably texting some celebrity her movie producer father had connected her to.

No hopes for Callie, who was so tame a kitten would probably scare her.

"It's so unhealthy," Merritt continued. "Not to mention gross. What guy would want to be on top of all of *that*?"

Tinsley let out a peal of laughter. "Or under it!"

"Enough," I thought. Or, at least, I thought I thought it.

The entire room quieted, and Merritt said, "What was that, *Aurora*?"

My shoulders tensed. "It's Rory."

"More like Borey," Poppy said.

I raised my eyebrows. "My name rhymes with whore and that's the best you can do? I expected more from you, Poppy."

Merritt seemed equally as unimpressed by Poppy's insult and held up a finger to stall Poppy's retort. "No, I want to hear what *Aurora* has to say. Tell me, how many guys have you been with?"

God, could everyone stop talking about my vagina for one hot second? "What's it matter? Just lay off."

"Oh, I get it, your feelings are hurt because you can't get a guy interested in all of...that."

I rolled my eyes. "Please. I could get a guy interested."

Okay, I might have been blowing hot air, but at this point, I'd do anything to get Merritt to shove her opinions up her size-zero ass.

"Oh, I'm sure you could get *a* guy interested. Chester would probably even pay you a quarter or two."

Tinsley cackled. "If he could get it up."

Poppy shrugged. "They make Viagra for a reason."

I bristled at them making fun of the sweet old

man who always hung out at Waldo's Café. Being insulted like that wasn't exactly fun either. Especially after the morning I'd had. "It's not like there's a checklist to get a guy to go out with you," I said. "They're free to choose who they want."

"And my point," Merritt said, walking toward my desk and swinging her pleated skirt on the way, "is that no hot guy in his right mind would go out with someone like...well...you."

I barely managed to keep my mouth shut. I'd heard Merritt talk like this to other people but had never had her wrath directed at me. (Being a teacher's kid had *some* advantages.) But now that I was an ant burning under Merritt's name-brand magnifying glass, I couldn't back down. Especially not with the other plus-sized girls overhearing this.

"I could get a hot guy to go out with me." I countered, sounding way more confident than I felt. Besides hotness was subjective, right?

"Oh?" She raised her eyebrows and looked around the room, lapping up the attention of everyone who had their eyes glued on us. "Did you all hear that? Precious Rory Hutton could get any guy she wanted."

More than a few people laughed along with her.

That didn't feel great, but I kept my eyes leveled at her. I was not backing down.

She pressed her manicured hands on my desk and leaned over, revealing her cleavage. "Do you mean it? Any guy and not just some hottie in a strait jacket?"

I stood up, not wanting to be underneath her in any way. "Really." I folded my arms over my chest, secretly wishing my mom would hurry up and get done grilling Dr. Edmonson about my prognosis.

"Prove it," she said.

"Oh yeah." I rolled my eyes. "Let me go grab a guy and ask him out with everyone watching. Good plan, Merritt."

She tapped her chin with a hot-pink fingernail. "Actually..."

I did not like the look flashing in her eyes. Not one bit.

"What do you say we make this interesting?"

I lifted an eyebrow. "Interesting?"

"Yeah." She crossed her arms, giving her push-up bra some help. "What do you say we make a bet?"

"Go on," I said, trying to hide my apprehension.

"If you can get Beckett Langley to take you to homecoming, I will gladly give up my homecoming crown and back off. If you lose, you stay home from homecoming. I don't need *your kind* ruining my day."

I rolled my eyes. "If you're going to make a bet, at least make it fair. I'm not trying to steal your boyfriend."

"He's not my boyfriend anymore." She leaned back on Jordan's desk, oblivious to the obvious discomfort on Jordan's face. Merritt picked at her nails, pretending to be bored, but I didn't miss the flash of pain that crossed her dainty features. "So what do you say? Do we have a deal?"

Jordan shifted back and gave me a look somewhere between upset and helpless. She wouldn't dare go up against Merritt and risk her scholarship.

It was up to me. "Game on."

The entire class gasped. Or maybe that was the blood rushing in my head.

I dropped into my chair, shell-shocked. Merritt forbid anyone in the room from saying a word of the bet until homecoming, on the threat of her daddy throwing around his money to get them kicked out of the school. It had been done before.

Mom came back minutes before the bell rang and assigned us chapters to read. At class change, I rushed to the hallway with the rest of the students, not wanting to hear what was sure to be a barrage of a million questions from my mother.

No, I had to get out of here and figure out how to do the impossible: get Beckett Langley to fall for a girl like me.

* * *

Continue reading Rory's story in Curvy Girls Can't Date Quarterbacks!

Use this code to discover Curvy Girls
Can't Date Quarterbacks!

ALSO BY KELSIE STELTING

Abi and the Boy She Loves: Book Three

The Pen Pal Romance Series

Dear Adam

Fabio Vs. the Friend Zone

Sincerely Cinderella

The Sweet Water High Series: A Multi-Author Collaboration

Road Trip with the Enemy: A Sweet Standalone Romance

YA Contemporary Romance Anthology

The Art of Taking Chances

Nonfiction

Raising the West

AUTHOR'S NOTE

Writing the final book of Abi's story was completely surreal. Part of me wanted to continue her saga and watch her and Jon grow their family, see them become successful professionals, and even face future challenges with her parents as they complete their prison sentences. But ending it here just feels right.

This entire series has been about Abi finding her identity outside of trauma and coming to form healthy relationships when all she's ever known is hurt, manipulation, and disappointment. A question I frequently get from readers is how much of myself goes into my stories. The short answer is all of it. The long answer is that I weave my hopes, dreams, and hurts into other worlds where I can mold them, shape them, and understand them.

When you've had trauma in your past, you are forced to take a look at yourself and ask how much of my current pain is my own doing? How many of my decisions are being made by my wounds and not by my wishes? It's hard to do, and I think Abi realizes that in this story.

Jon's proposal threw her for a complete loop. There she was, getting everything she'd ever dreamt of, but it wasn't right. If she was going to be true to herself and the type of life she wanted to live, she had to say no. I believe saying no was the best thing she could have said—for both of them.

They learned how to heal, and were forced to look at the kind of life they wanted to live. I've stayed in Abi's head most of this series, but I imagine that was a dark time for Jon. I'm proud of him for growing and becoming the man Abi deserved!

We all have some chips around the edges and some pain we haven't let go of. At least, I know I do. As you're reading this, I challenge you to ask yourself —what wound has been making decisions for you, and how can you heal it?

My prayer is that you'll come to love yourself in

your beautifully broken form as you take the pieces of your hurt and put them back together into the new image of you.

ACKNOWLEDGMENTS

As always, thank you to my readers who have been the most supporting, loving crew of people I (or Abi) could have asked for! I love talking with you as Abi grows and hearing your reactions to each story! Special thanks to Laurie, Shelia, Abbey, Dixie, Wanda, Texas, and other readers who have beta read each book and looked deep into the heart of the story! I appreciate you!

Sally Henson, thank you for being a fabulous friend and sounding board.

Tricia Harden, this is our sixth book together! Skye two and three, Road Trip with the Enemy, and Abi's entire series would not be the same without you. I love working with you and hope to do so for years to come!

Anne-Marie Meyer, thank you for advising me on book descriptions and covers! Your tenacity and eye for details is inspiring.

Everyone owes my mother a massive thank you for always asking me if I'm writing. (I suppose I do too.)

I've had many people comment on my characters getting married young. I think you have my husband/high school sweetheart to blame for that. Ty, thank you for your sunshine smile and loving me through all the brokenness. You are great inspiration for a loving man who knows how to grow and support someone no matter what. It hasn't been easy, but it has always been worth it.

Thank you to my family, who may not be able to keep up with each story but never miss a chance to support me or spread the word. I love each of you more than you know.

To everyone who's been with Abi since release day of book one or recent readers, I appreciate the time you spend with Abi more than words can say. I pray you have loved every second.

Kelsie Stelting is a body positive romance author who writes love stories with strong characters, deep feelings, and happy endings.

She currently lives in Colorado. You can often find her writing, spending time with family, and soaking up too much sun wherever she can find it.

Visit www.kelsiestelting.com to get a

free story and sign up for her readers' group!

facebook.com/kelsiesteltingcreative

twitter.com/kelsiestelting

instagram.com/kelsiestelting